Children of the Black Sabbath

Also by Anne Hébert

The Silent Rooms
Kamouraska
Poems

Children of the Black Sabbath

Anne Hébert

Translated by Carol Dunlop-Hébert

PaperJacks LTD.

Markham, Ontario, Canada

A CANADIAN

PaperJacks

One of a series of Canadian books
published by PaperJacks Ltd.

CHILDREN OF THE BLACK SABBATH

Musson Book Company edition published October, 1977

PaperJacks edition published June, 1978

 PaperJacks editions are published by PaperJacks Ltd., 330 Steelcase Road, Markham, Ontario L3R 2M1.

ISBN 0-7701-0073-2

First published as *Les enfants du sabbat*
by Editions du Seuil

Printed in Canada

Children of the Black Sabbath

As long as the vision lasted, Sister Julie of the Trinity, lady of the Precious Blood, motionless in her cell, her arms folded on her chest, in all the width and stiffness of her habit, examined the shanty in detail, as though she would have to account for it on Judgement Day.

Never since she'd entered the convent had she permitted herself this kind of seeing: no longer stealthy, immediately suppressed, but deliberate and considered. So as to efface, forever, the obsessional image, to rid herself of that childhood shanty, clear it away once and for all. And above all, above all the rest, to free herself from the sacred pair who ruled the destiny of the shanty, somewhere out there on the mountain of B. . ., amidst the rocks, the tangled tree trunks, the stumps and the underbrush.

A man and a woman are standing in the doorway, smiling with their wide red mouths and white teeth. The sun, like a ball of fire about to topple behind the mountain, lights the sky, staining with pink the tanned hands of the man and the woman. A small boy opens his torn shorts, pisses very high, hitting the trunk of a pine whose top is lost in the sky, but aiming, in fact, at the dying sun.

His little sister admires him for it. Sitting on a woodpile, she rummages in her shock of hair tatted with straw, grass, and pine needles. Her brown neck, arms and legs are riddled with mosquito bites. The air is scented, ringing with insects and birds.

Sister Julie has a close view of the man, the woman and the two children; she sees them clearly and precisely. The light flooding the scene becomes exceedingly vulnerable, like some unique thing doomed to disappear. Fearing the unknown wound the light might inflict, Sister Julie begins to note the exact measurements of the shanty and take a methodical inventory of it, to calm herself.

Not imposing in size, the shanty consists of a series of additions that make it look like straggling wooden blocks, half swallowed by the forest, half askew, poorly joined, and set at different levels on large boulders that serve as a pile foundation. The main block (fifteen feet by twelve) can be recognized by its door, once red, now violet and pink. The two square windows on either side of the door are also trimmed in the same faded colour. Two worn wooden steps lead up to the door. The clapboard walls gleam silver grey, are soft to the touch, polished by rain, sun and snow, like a wreck one might find on the seashore.

Inside the main room, you are immediately overcome by a strong prevailing odour. There is salt pork sizzling steadily in the frying pan. Tobacco fumes float above the table. You can also distinguish the musky smell of the father and the mother, and the sharper odour of the two unkempt children, covered with fleas and filth. A blue washbasin of bruised enamel lies on the rough wooden floor, just beneath a black and rusting pump. In a corner, a few potatoes leak from a burlap sack.

"Spuds, spuds, everlastin' spuds!"

A woman's voice breaks in, mingles with the odour.

"Spuds, spuds, everlastin' spuds, and half spoilt to boot!"

And then the sizzle of the frying pan is no longer heard. No greasy smoke rises now, although the smell of the fried pork, and the even heavier smell of boiled pork, permeate, forever, the walls of fir and the half-stripped beams of the ceiling.

On the wall, spread wide round the nail upon which it rests, is a strange woman's hat of blue straw; entangled in it, the red and golden brass wires of a bird and a flower.

"I'm goin' to put my pretty red hat on my head 'n go downtown to Georgiana's. I'm fed up with eatin' spoilt spuds. If you don't want to work, Adélard, I'm goin' to have to. . . ."

While the threat of the mother's departure hovers in the kitchen and the father withdraws into his silence, you can escape by the back door. This ill-fitting door has a dazzling knob of white porcelain.

Once the door is open, you have only to follow the uncovered plank footbridge that leads to the summer rooms. Precariously laid on stones of different heights, its ups and downs seem to roll beneath your feet. You can glimpse the beaten earth between the disjointed boards. Now and then a long green snake will suddenly uncoil itself below and disappear, with a sound like rustling cloth, among the rust-coloured ferns and wild rhubarb that line the passageway.

Small and windowless, the two rooms are in fact more like airtight boxes. On the wall are long strips of bark that the children playfully rip with their penknives.

The bed, with the elaborate curlicues of its iron frame, takes up all the space in the parents' room. The mattress rises in abrupt bumps like boulders under the thickness of the red and violet patchwork quilt.

The children sleep on straw pallets on the floor, happy to come back each evening to their own smell mingled with the stale, prickly, filthy straw. They huddle together as if in the belly of a rough and familiar beast. Sometimes they even bury their heads in it, at the risk of suffocating.

The only way out of the children's room is through that of the parents. And when the mother and father go on a fling that lasts the whole day long, the children are stuck in their room until the next day.

Sister Julie shares the children's anguish. She catches herself saying, with the little girl (suddenly blending into one and the same being with the little girl),

"Ain't they ever goin' to finish! Oh Jesus! Ain't they ever goin' to finish!"

But Sister Julie is powerless to block out the rumpus of caresses and blows coming from the other side of the partition.

When she has to go through her parents' room, there is no longer anyone there. The room is empty, to her great relief and sadness. The enormous bed, its patchwork quilt half burst open, occupies the place of honour.

A door cut into the partition is open and looks out on the shed.

Once there were rabbits in the shed, crowded into cages, and hens that pecked freely at the straw. But there is nothing living left here, just old hay and soiled straw. In a corner, an earthen vat full of wilting herbs planted in close rows. In times past, you had only to push the straw from underfoot to uncover the iron ring and the trap door.

The same light that, before, illuminated the shanty under the tree (the light coming from Sister Julie's head, like a spotlight) is now shed on the wooden ladder and the cellar with its stone walls tainted by a green and muddy moss, like that seen on rocks in the midst of mountain streams.

In such a crude light, you can't help noticing the smooth operation of the still, in perfect running order, with its smoking chimney, its worm, its boiler filled with firewood. A strange and joyous liquid simmers softly. On the ground, logs lie about.

The moonshiners can't be far off.

On a long plank set on sawhorses, in a row: bottles, glass jugs and a tin funnel.

The light dims little by little. Sister Julie has just time to examine one of the empty jugs. A glass jug like those in which vinegar is sold. One can still read the green label: *One of the Heinz 57 varieties.*

The light disappears completely. You are plunged into darkness. The still whistles and hisses lustily.

A heavy cautious step approaches the shanty. Someone's fingernails scratch against the door panel. A man's voice, imperious yet imploring, mutters the password.

"La Goglue, you there?"

A woman stirs in the shadow of the cellar. Impossible to glimpse her face. She pours a liquid into one of the jugs bearing the green deceitful label. Her husband is behind her, watching over the operation. He laughs. While the man outside, against the door, becomes impatient, demands his gallon of moonshine. He roars now:

"La Goglue, you there?"

Sister Julie recovers consciousness suddenly, in the bareness of her cell. Not as though she had slept and dreamt, but as if something real and extremely precise had just faded away before her. She is left with an intense impression of loss. In a shanty, somewhere on a mountain, someone hungers for her, far more than God ever hungered after her soul. And Sister Julie, too, is starving for what lies hidden on the mountain. More than for her entire life in the convent. More even than for God Himself.

She feels a sharp pain in her head and in the nape of her neck.

The small owl's head turns stiffly on the wide white neck. Sister Julie of the Trinity stares straight ahead at the doctor. She sees her own reflection in his huge horn-rimmed glasses; Sister Julie contemplates the garment of her mortification. Bits of straight hair straggle from under her cloth headband. The hospital gown stops at her knees and gapes at the back to reveal Sister Julie's rounded buttocks.

The question, the real question that would wrench the true answer from my body like a pulled tooth. To bare my reality, expel it from between my ribs. My whole heart. No, none of these little inquisitive people will ever be able to tear the slightest fragment of truth from me. They shan't take me alive. Let them talk and ask their endless questions; they don't know what they're after. And if ever they did corner me in my ultimate refuge, probe my loins and my heart with subtle instruments, they wouldn't believe what they heard or saw. This one's been talking for quite a while now. His flat voice drones at the very edge of my patience. A disgusting litany of urine and blood, excrements, bowels made visible by barium, a skeleton seen through skin and flesh, a scalped skull bared to the bone by x-rays.

"You're in perfect health, Sister."

"I can't bear the coif any longer. It scorches me like flames. Our Mother Superior will tell you. With her own eyes she's seen the red marks on my neck and my forehead and nape. It's like being caught in a vise. Horrible iron tongs . . ."

"You're extremely nervous, Sister. Have you noticed if the migraines start with your period?"

Sister Julie stares straight ahead. Her entire face seems to turn to stone. Her yellow eye widens and freezes. Her lips tighten. She lifts a hand to her forehead: it's a child's hand, short-nailed and robust like that of a small boy.

"I almost always have a headache. But as the date fixed for my profession grows near, it becomes intolerable. It's as though my bones were cracking. I can't move my shoulders or turn my head. . . ."

"You have a vivid imagination, Sister."

"I've already had to put off my vows twice."

"What does your Mother Superior have to say about this?"

"That it is a temptation of the devil, and I must pray constantly."

"You can always pray, Sister. It can't do you any harm. But you also need vitamins and fresh air. Don't forget to open the window whenever possible, and to take good deep breaths. And drink milk, lots of milk."

What a lovely prescription; we might just as well tack it up over our bed, like a holy picture. As for opening the window, the Mother Superior forbids it.

The Mother Superior's voice, almost subterranean, insinuates itself somewhere near Sister Julie's shoulder.

"One never knows what the outside air might bring in, hidden in a speck of dust, in a cinder. The devil is sly and insidious, like a grain of sand."

The doctor again.

"You may leave the hospital, Sister. I'm giving you your discharge. Don't forget: fresh air, pasteurized milk, iron and vitamin C. No coffee or tea. With quiet and good humour, all will be fine."

You must consider yourself cured, or rather demystified, reduced to the simplest expression, rid of false pains and the parody of despair.

Leave the hospital as soon as possible, so they'll stop turning her over and over every which way like a dubious object, stop suspecting some defect of blood or bones; so she will no longer have to dread an open-heart operation, but be able to look upon her prison with her secret still intact, and dress without the help of any mirror, her movements as accurate as those of the blind, don once again the black robe of the ladies of the Precious Blood, the scapular, the wimple and the white linen coif, her white novice's veil, her rosary hanging on her belt of rope. And await the profession of her perpetual vows.

No, the coif isn't burning me yet, but I can already feel it along my cheeks, as if it were drawn on my skin with a very fine penknife lightly pressed.

"Are you coming, Sister? The convent car is waiting for us. You're sure you haven't forgotten anything?"

Sister Gemma, beaming with joy, noisily goes about opening and closing the metal drawers. Now quite agitated, she lays a black cape, worn but carefully mended, on Sister Julie's shoulders. Her high-pitched voice exults:

"Well, Sister, you've nothing at all, not the slightest illness. The doctor said so. You must be glad to be in perfect health?"

The cape is heavy as lead on my shoulders. Sister Geneviève of the Holy Face wore it until her death. I inherited it with its pervasive odour of an elderly sick nun.

Their hands tucked into their sleeves, their skirts spread wide over the seat of the car, the two sisters prepare to cross the city.

The streets are open, people are out. Men, women and children. Large stretches of sun. Neatly drawn spots of shade. The world is clear and precise. The sky incredibly blue. Now and then, a sign inciting us to subscribe to the victory loan. It's summer. There are cars lined up along the sidewalks, others speeding along. A moving, colourful day. Flash. Rapid flashes. Fragments of life whirl about the sisters' car. A host of ephemera. The windows are shut tight.

Sister Gemma casts furtive glances. Her homely ivory-coloured face lights up brightly at every passing store window.

Sister Julie tightens her fists inside the large sleeves.

I don't have the energy, or even the wish, to cast a glance sideways through my coif. This is surely the way God wants it, so that I may renounce the world in every image the city offers. Now all I have to do is go blind about the world and continue to believe in the possible shadow of God. Farther on, perhaps? At the end of the road, after crossing the entire span of life and death.

Beyond the city walls. The Grande Allée. A house of cut stone, isolated from its neighbours, draws Sister Julie. In front of the strange house, she freezes.

Sister Julie doesn't appear to be lost in dream. On the contrary, her entire person, swaddled in cloth and linen, seems to be in a state of acute awareness. In vain she defends herself against the earth of the garden, barely glimpsed, against the trees, against the silent dwelling.

Seemingly continuing to recite her beads to herself, Sister Gemma murmurs in Sister Julie's ear:

"They say that Maître Talbot never behaved very well with his wife. He's always been hard on her. And they say the poor woman is very ill."

Sister Julie knows this: inside the closed house, in one

of the upstairs rooms, a thin chalk-white skeleton peaks through an ever more transparent skin. Sister Julie crosses herself stealthily, a light tap of the thumb on her breast. Too late. Obscure forces have captured her entire person, have lured her inside the Talbot house, placed her in the presence of the intolerable event upstairs. Sister Julie, standing beside the dying woman like an indispensable witness, hastens to announce the news.

Leaning towards Sister Gemma, she speaks very softly without moving her head and with no visible parting of her lips:

"We must pray, Sister Gemma, immediately, very hard. Madame Talbot is dying."

I aspire only to taking my vows as soon as possible. Once I've reached the point of no return I'll be saved. I ask just one thing of God: to become a nun like the others for all eternity; to lose myself among the others and no longer show the slightest singularity. A small interchangeable nun among other small interchangeable nuns lined up two by two: the same habit, the same gestures, the same little metal-rimmed eyeglasses. Yes, I'll even wear them if you require, even if my sight is piercing. False teeth too, if you wish, even if my own are solid and brilliant. A smooth face expressing neither joy nor sorrow, evened out, filed down, obliterated.

Madame Talbot died at the precise hour and the very moment at which Sister Julie announced her death to Sister Gemma. Trembling, Sister Gemma whispers this to her companions.

A slap of the clapper brings the sisters' recess murmurs

to an abrupt end. The rule is formal. Any word crossing the wall of silence, at the times and places permitted and reserved for that use, must be pronounced clearly and intelligibly, to the edification of the greatest possible number of our sisters. Private or whispered conversations are strictly forbidden.

The Mother Superior quickly reminds Sister Gemma that our Holy Mother Church, in its infinite wisdom, recommends the utmost caution concerning the supernatural interpretation of certain extraordinary phenomena. She decides to question Sister Julie immediately.

From behind her desk Mother Marie-Clotilde of the Cross examines Sister Julie with inordinate attention.

Sister Julie lowers her head; she'd like to hide her face in her hands.

Mother Marie-Clotilde doesn't take her eyes off Sister Julie.

I am the Superior here, I am in charge of these young girls. I say to one: go, and she goes; to another: come, and she comes; and to the new postulant who enters this house: do this, and she does it. Is it not essential that each of my daughters, without exception, present herself before me like an open book, so that I may easily read her soul? Such is my duty as Superior and spiritual director. But this little Sister Julie, what a thorn in my side! Her soul steals away before me. The composed and sullen, almost stealthy, look on her face now, something feigned . . .

"The doctor's report is categorical. You are sound of mind and body. It's your soul that is sick, dangerously sick. We are going to try, by the grace of God, to hasten your recovery."

Sister Julie remains silent. She shuts her eyes as though she'd fallen asleep standing up and in full armour.

"Sister, do you realize that you can lie to me by not answering, by remaining silent?"

"The chaplain told me."

"What keeps you from unburdening your soul now?

Confess, my daughter. Make a clean breast of it, and be delivered. You'll be able to pronounce your vows, your soul at peace, at the next taking of vows. Admit that your supposed revelations are only idle talk and stories you tell your companions to make yourself interesting? Admit that your supposed pains are play-acting?"

Sister Julie persists in her silence, her fingernails gouging her palms.

"Your thoughts, Sister? How do you want God to help you, if you refuse to open your soul to me, your Superior?"

Sister Julie decides to speak. It's a thin, bland voice that doesn't seem to belong to her.

"I pledge before you, Mother, never to complain again of any ache or pain, never to believe in any presentiment and to accomplish my duties faithfully. . . ."

"Our Holy Rule is there to help you. Be faithful in the smallest details, and God will do the rest. You must banish forever these simulated illnesses and illuminations of which you've been the victim and accomplice. Stop indulging in self-pity. Above all, don't trust yourself. You must, do you hear, must give yourself over to the strictest obedience. It's your last chance. If you don't pronounce your final vows in September at the next taking of the habit, you are lost. I can do no more for you. Our convent will reject you and the world will take you back, undoubtedly to your own damnation. A nun who fails her vocation has no easy time finding peace in this world or the other. Your silence is harder than a stone wall, my Sister. How do you think I can help you? You refuse all help. You discourage the best of good wills."

Once again, Sister Julie's silence, unreal, ironical.

"I'll do what you tell me, Mother."

"You should confess as soon as possible, my daughter. With the help of God the chaplain will perhaps deliver you of your secret."

"I promise to go to confession, Mother."

"Kneel, my daughter, that I may bless you."

Sister Julie kneels on the floor. At the Superior's feet. Sister Julie's face is now only the crooked bridge of a nose and wide lowered eyelids; you wouldn't suspect the roundness of her cheeks, pinched by the white linen coif.

Mother Marie-Clotilde's firm hand traces the sign of the cross on Sister Julie's bowed head.

Sister Julie, her two knees on the floor, sinks into contemplation of the polished parquetry. Her head spins. The floor shines and its pattern swells unduly, carries Sister Julie off in its dazzle, swallows her mind. Vertigo.

Suddenly there is a pail full of Javel water on the floor. A second Mother Marie-Clotilde comes out of the first, leaves the chair, approaches Sister Julie noiselessly, kneels down beside her. Sister Julie is already scrubbing the floor as ordered. The Superior dips the floorcloth in the pail and without wringing it slowly bathes Sister Julie's face. It is extraordinarily painful and voluptuous. While all around her the floor peels and roughens, full of splinters.

"My daughters' faces must be scrubbed like a bright and shining floor,"

snickers an unrecognizable voice.

Sister Julie lifts her head sharply. The Superior doesn't appear to have moved. She's still in place on her chair behind her desk, her hand raised to bless Sister Julie, indefinitely one might think. But her stomach heaves as though Sister Julie, kneeling at her feet, had acted out some indecent scene before her, something extremely incriminating for the Superior and the entire community.

Sister Julie already dreads the moment when she will have to confess her visions, like sins.

"What are your thoughts, Sister? I order you to answer me."

"I have none, Mother. None, I assure you."

Mother Marie-Clotilde's wide face. Her darting, frightened but handsome horse's eyes, enlarged by the eyeglass lenses, remain fixed upon Sister Julie, without lashes or any shadow. The entire person of Mother Marie-Clotilde is given over to an exhausting curiosity.

"Get up, my daughter. Our chaplain will find a way to loosen your tongue. He'll hear your confession."

Sister Julie straightens up with a brutal start. She looks Mother Marie-Clotilde straight in the eye.

My face to read, Mother, hard and smooth, a perfect pebble. May my Mother Superior read on it what is hers by right: obedience, submission. But as for the darkest core of my heart, my most shadowed night, my secret vocation, may my Mother Superior whet her curiosity in vain. It's my life I'm defending. I'm sure I'm defending my life.

Sister Julie's voice, this time ringing, almost triumphant:

"I'll go to confession, Mother, since you order me to. The chaplain is expecting me. I'm certain he's waiting for me. It's time."

Sister Julie leaves the room with long strides.

Mother Marie-Clotilde is left straight and standing. She contemplates her large hands with stupefaction, as if they were separated from her body: they are trembling with fury.

Sister Julie breaks into a run. Three corridors and two stairways aren't enough to exhaust her energy. It's as though a gale were driving her along, a bundle of sails set out to sea.

Never before has the holy habit seemed so easy to handle, so supple; it's like flying.

Sister Julie slows her pace on approaching the chapel. Once again her skirts hang heavy, her coif is tight on her head, along her cheeks.

I promised to remain in the convent until the end of my life. I promised. To submit to the rules, obey the law. I promised.

Now Sister Julie must drag herself forward. With every step she encounters a strange resistance in the air. With her knees and thighs she pushes up the compact mass of her leaden skirts.

I am walking for my brother Joseph, who's off at the

war. Each step I take demands such an effort. I want to believe in the communion of saints. Let Joseph rest a bit while I painfully place one foot in front of the other. Let him seize the chance to sit down beside the road, near a ditch perhaps, or in the shade of a wall. Let him lay down his pack beside him on the cool grass. Take a drink of water from the canteen hanging at his belt. And in the meantime I'll try to read between the English words stamped on all the letters I've received from him. *Somewhere at the front*. Try to see how his face looks now. A three-day-old beard, probably. Sweat running down his cheeks. The handsomest of mankind's children. He's lost weight. I'm sure he's lost weight. He's thinner than Christ on the cross. And I adore him, secretly. I know it's a sacrilege. Let no prophet presume to number his bones. I alone have that right. My hand will brush lightly over his skeleton, sensitive under the stretched and naked skin. I'll ease his every pain. Place my fingers like a balm in his wounded heart. The blow dealt by a German soldier. I'll sew up the wound with my fingers. Take on all his sufferings. His horrible thirst scorches me already. I'll go without drinking. I'll wear a hair-shirt and the spiked bracelet. I will obey until death. So long as he lives! May he cross the fire of war unscathed. I want him to live! Without pain or injury. To be alive as no one has ever been alive in the world of the living. Avoid sleep. Don't drink anymore. Don't eat anymore. Take his place through all those wartime trials. Be cold for him. Be afraid. Receive the bullets and blows destined for him. Be taken prisoner in his place. My liberty has been rotting on the spot for three years now in this convent. For him! Him, him alone! My beloved brother!

Lighthearted, her soul appeased, she runs to her confessor. With no trace of that passionate ecstasy during which her brother Joseph once again took the place of God.

"I confess my sins to God and before you, Father. It's

been a week since my last confession. I received absolution and did my penance."

The worn soles of Sister Julie's shoes can be seen under the small violet curtain of the confessional for a long time.

Father Migneault explains to Sister Julie that she continually lies without knowing it. Her deepest nature is false, perverted as it were. And that explains her supposed revelations and visions as well as the imaginary illnesses from which she suffers. Father Migneault pronounces the words as though exhausted, crushed under the weight of the convent's sins, and the sins of the entire world. He lowers his head, with a gesture of fatigue, against the grille separating him from Sister Julie. And for a brief moment, his moist forehead touches Sister Julie's cheek.

"In the name of the Father, the Son and the Holy Ghost, I absolve you of your sins. For your penance you will recite ten Our Fathers and ten Hail Marys on your knees, your arms extended as on the cross. Go in peace, and pray God to deliver you from imposture!"

The little chapel, white and gilded.

May I form a standing cross with all my aching body! May not one joint flinch or crack. God Himself cannot ask for more. Reduced to my cross-like form, completely given over to the physical effort of remaining like a cross, I haven't time to think about myself or the world or God or my brother Joseph. No one. Nothing. Only my body remains. In my head, a rigorous bookkeeping. Keep an accurate account of the Our Fathers and the Hail Marys. Above all keep my arms up. Stare straight ahead at the sanctuary lamp, sign of God's true presence in the tabernacle. It's like meeting God face to face, unblinking, only to realize that I have nothing to say to Him. This is how absolutely poor, completely destitute I am. All my energy concentrated on one point. Remain a cross for the prescribed time. Perhaps God, hidden in the tabernacle, is facing me in just the same way in the silence of His cross, at the moment of His own most total solitude, forsaken.

Too long an absence. The more Christ appears to her as the Solitary and Abandoned One, invisible behind his purple curtain, the deeper Sister Julie sinks into her melancholy, conscious of the futility of her sacrifice. And the greater Sister Julie's sadness and depression, the greater the temptation to welcome the magical consolation that comes to her from the shanty and from the entire mountain of B. . . .

Now she no longer feels the painful tension of her two outstretched arms. The exhaustion of her crucified body is changed to a strange softness. Muscles, nerves and joints all relax. Her heart beats slowly, like a sleeper's heart. Only the extraordinary sharpness of her intensified senses links Sister Julie with the living.

In spite of the distance she clearly hears the fluttering sound of the flame in the sanctuary lamp. The revelation of this secret music fills her with joy. But now her gladness knows no bounds: she perceives (with her eyes, her hands, her ears, her parted lips; with her skin, which is exceedingly sensitive all over, as if she were naked) a very strong wind, gushing like a sudden draft from the other end of the chapel, near the door. While the elderly nun who prays leaning against a pillar just two steps away from Sister Julie seems to notice nothing.

The violent wind dies down upon approaching the altar and spends itself in a murmur like a human breath, snuffing with a single gust the sanctuary lamp.

Sister Julie of the Trinity's spirit is carried off to the mountain, while her body remains standing like a cross, like a stone Calvary. In the white and gilded chapel of the ladies of the Precious Blood.

A woman, wearing a pink dress and a blue straw hat trimmed with a flower and a bird, climbs briskly up the abrupt rise of sand and stone towards the shanty. She hauls two enormous yellow cardboard suitcases, breathing rapidly, smiling broadly.

Her breathing and smile fill Sister Julie with pleasure. Were she to put out her hand she'd touch the woman's mouth and teeth and taste her salty breath.

Sister Julie knows that the woman is coming back from the city after a stay at Georgiana's. She also knows that the man is up there on the threshold of the shanty, waiting for her.

The two children sit in the sand pretending to play. But they are really hoping with all their hearts for the scene about to take place between the mother and the father, the reconciliation and the opening of the suitcase brimming with presents.

But the children are looking forward to the water ceremony even more than to the presents.

Very softly, as though reciting a raging prayer, the father says to the mother:

"Get out, you pig, you slut, I want no more of your pig's hide in my house."

The father stands in the shanty door, blocking her passage.

The mother is still laughing but she doesn't dare go any farther. She's set her suitcases down on the ground. She knows exactly what's coming to her. Her arms hanging loose, she looks at the father. Patient and motionless, smiling still, she accepts her punishment.

The man's tiny eyes shine. Malice and pleasure are so perfectly balanced between the man and the woman that you can't help believing that justice and love will be given to each according to his works, glaringly, totally.

Now the father has placed the mother against the shanty wall, beside the brimming rain barrel. He begins at once to wash her, new clothes and all. Joyfully he pours pails and pails of water and mud over her head and body.

The dress and underclothes instantly cling to the woman's body like slimy seaweed. Her yellow permanent droops. A few corkscrew curls dribble down her face and neck. She screams that all her new booty is going to be ruined. She shivers. Cries out with little yelps and coughs, half drowned.

The man runs off to fetch the quilt on the big iron bed and wraps his wife in it. He wipes her face and head and feet with his handkerchief, kisses her tenderly on the behind and takes her, soaking wet, rolled up in the quilt, in his arms. Swoops into the shanty with his burden, who has already begun chuckling through her tears.

The children approach the suitcases and take stock of the presents their mother has brought back from the city.

The parents didn't reappear for three days. Then they stretched and yawned on the threshold. In the dazzling sun. They were very hungry. With their white teeth and ravaged mouths, you might have thought they were two ogres.

The procession of nuns has set off along the corridors and stairways with lowered eyes and noiseless tread.

Sister Gemma, the vestry nun, bustles about preparing the altar and the mass.

Sister Julie is still on her knees, her arms extended, winding up the Hail Marys and the Our Fathers of her penance with no signs of fatigue, except for a very slight weakening of the arms. On her pale face, a vague, evil gleam.

Fear suddenly grasps Sister Gemma. The sanctuary lamp, although filled with oil, has gone out. In spite of the fact that not the slightest breath of air troubles the hermetic convent.

On the street side, the grey, rough stone surface. Bars on the windows. The heavy door of solid wood opens and closes, solemn and slow. It isn't that the door squeaks on its well-oiled hinges, but if you touch it the least bit there is a stifled sound of massive wood that reverberates in an endless echo. On the kitchen side, a low door looks out on the courtyard. There's a small opening in the courtyard wall near the kitchen, a grey painted door, but it's kept carefully locked. The key hangs on a ring from the Sister Cook's belt all day long. Our Holy Rule commands her to give the key to the Mother Superior each night, along with the keys to the vegetable cellar, the cold storage room and all the kitchen cupboards.

Each year brings us a fresh batch of hand-picked postulants. One, two, sometimes three girls in a family are set aside. The city sends its share, but most of our nuns come from the country.

Time flows over us drop by drop as over a bare wall on which obedience commands us to draw the Passion of the Saviour with precise strokes. Nothing's missing. Not the nails or the whips or the crown of thorns, or the blow of the spear or the perfect complicity which makes us victims as well as tormentors.

Asperges me Domine . . .

Thou shalt sprinkle me with hyssop and I will be whiter than snow.

Movement and voice are given back to us. The sound of the clapper. Stand. Sit. Kneel. Genuflection. A large sign of the cross. Small crosses on the forehead, mouth and breast. Lower our heads. Raise our heads. The solemn ballet of the mass. A sunbeam sets aglow the green vestments embroidered in gold.

Dominus vobiscum.

I'm distracted, like someone listening to two conversations at once. I hear the words of the mass. I sing the words of the mass. I go through all the prescribed movements in perfect synchronization with my sisters. Yet I strongly feel the presence of the man and the woman of the mountain; they prowl about me. The air becomes rarified in the entire chapel, as though pumped out by some preposterous creatures. The man's name is Adélard, the woman's Philomène, called La Goglue. I know they're here. They're strolling about the aisles, shoving each other, stretching out on the empty pews.

Now they've settled on the altar, just beside the Tabernacle. I see their bright eyes, like little black lamps. The atmosphere is unbreathable. I'm choking. They're so near me I could touch them. Their enormous breath fills the whole chapel. I'm amazed that our sisters, deprived of air, don't keel over row after row like a field of winged cornets before the scythe.

Someone is approaching me, and while the air thickens, becomes visible as she grows near: Philomène. Her round breasts, her splendid rump, her cheerful yellow head held high, her pink dress. A mirthful man holds a church canopy with one raised hand above the woman's head. I hear them laughing. I'd like to cover my ears and close my eyes and let Philomène and Adélard disappear.

But I go on looking and hearing. I can't prevent it. What surprises me most is the indifference of our sisters and the celebrant. They don't seem to realize what's happening. I alone have the gift of sight; I alone am violently torn out of my own body.

The two filthy, naked children have stayed in the background near the door, leaning against the holy water basin.

Now they trot up the aisle and pass very close to me, hand in hand. They greet me with friendly gestures. The little girl leans towards me. Her beady yellow eyes embarrass me like a mirror. Her tart voice.

"You should be ashamed. We're like two peas in a pod. You're me and I'm you. And you pretend to be a nun!"

It would be easy to take by the arm the little girl who's taunting me and drag her off to confession. Let her confess all her sins to Father Migneault! That way I'd be delivered, absolved, white as snow, cleansed of childhood and future. Convent life would close in around me like the dead water of a stagnant pool.

Perhaps I fear drowning in that pool. And the little girl's signs, inciting me to follow her right up to the altar where the father and mother are plotting some secret they alone know, are so inviting. The parents crunch away on the sacred hosts as though they were soda crackers. While our sisters intone with their sweet, bland voices:

Mea culpa, mea maxima culpa.

"What you got cooking there, woman? Something smells terrible. Company coming?"

"You're not keen on country smells, dear husband?"

Before Adélard's gleeful eye, Philomène has just added some fresh guano to the mixture brewing in a pot on the stove. She turns to Adélard, spoon in hand. They both laugh so hard the earth surrounding the shanty seems about to split open and rise up in swirls of dust.

The aroma of warm alcohol greets Adélard in the cellar. Inebriated by the odour alone, he goes about preparing the whisky blanc for the festivities.

Drops of liquid drip from the still and fall one by one into a tin pitcher with a sound as regular as that of a metronome.

Once the pitcher is full Adélard empties it into one of the glass jugs he's been keeping ready. He carefully bottles this essence of drunkenness, soul and spirit of the drink. While Philomène recovers the thick froth and pungent bitterness that have formed on the surface of the tub. The woman gathers up all that hasn't been brewed or passed through the still. She pulverizes, reduces, stirs and blends the residue in the pot on the stove, in which a slick, greasy unguent of strange herbs, rare mushrooms and obscure debris has almost finished simmering.

"Most people wants to celebrate the worst way!" says Adélard.

"Goin' to get mighty private invitations," says Philomène.

She doesn't trust the village people who live down there in the hollow beside the river, nestled about the church and its priest like a frightened school of fish. Only the few faithful among them, the trustworthy accomplices who regularly steal away from the village after nightfall to climb the rise leading to the shanty in quest of a few gallons of alcohol will be admitted to the festivities. As for the others, they'll have to win them over little by little, continue to look after and cure them, suck them in from time to time with the odd little miracle, something to do with the weather or the elements, before daring to invite them to the sabbat.

The prize guests, the best of the greedy feasters, creatures of desire and deprivation, are city people who've been steeped in the humiliation of unemployment. Philomène spotted them during her last stay at Georgiana's in Quebec City.

The old Fords salvaged from the junkyard are already underway. Paper roses stuck into glass flutes, shades drawn to protect against the brightness of the following car's headlights. Clouds of dust. One complains of sand between his teeth, as though he were eating spinach. On either side of the road the shrilling of crickets accompanies the cortege of cars up the mountain of B. . . .

The cars must be carefully hidden at a safe distance from the shanty, parked as far away as possible, behind brushwood patches on forgotten trails.

The shanty can't accommodate so many at a time. The guests overflow from it, spread outside amidst the mosquitoes and the song of frogs.

A woman whispers the latest news; indignation mingles with a mystical fright.

"The cardinal has banned dancing in the entire diocese of Quebec."

Philomène claims she heard the crash in New York a while ago. A sinister crunching. Or rather a tearing sound like a hundred linen sheets suddenly rent from top to bottom. A skyscraper sinking into the Hudson River.

"It set my teeth on edge! A terrible sound!"

A man reads a newspaper out loud, distinctly pronouncing each syllable:

June 12, 1930. Never has there been so much stagnation and unemployment. Mannion declares . . . It seems that in some taverns you can exchange a tramway ticket for a glass of beer. Montreal has $400,000,000 to provide food, drink and lodging to the unfortunate . . . The Meurling Refuge is open.

A man talks of the "back to the land" movement. A woman cries and says that going back to the land means nothing but lying under it with six feet of earth on top.

Philomène eyes her son and daughter and declares with a throaty laugh:

"This is my body and my blood!"

Everybody laughs, their mouths gaping too widely.

The children are afraid they'll be eaten and drunk, changed into bread and wine in a world where food is scarce, the unemployed voracious, and the powers of Philomène and Adélard far greater than those of the priest at mass.

Philomène assures them there'll be enough food and drink for all.

"Blessed are they that hunger and thirst, for they shall be filled."

The men have already begun drinking directly from the jug that Adélard passes around. They choke, spit and spatter themselves. The women also start in, passing a tin goblet around among them. They're heard to say it burns like fire.

Dominus vobiscum
Et cum spiritu tuo
Sursum corda
Oremus.

Sister Julie is ecstatic and white in the chapel; she appears to sleep in her pew. While in reality she's already begun to descend to the bottom of the ravine in the heart of the forest.

It's no use trying to hold on by the tufts of grass or the rare rootless bushes; they come away in your hand with a cloud of sand and dry clods. Better to let yourself slide down to the bottom without grabbing anything.

Full moon.

The bottom of the ravine had been cleared and stumped. Only a few fir and larch trees remain.

The three magic circles are marked off with close-set stones. The first circle goes round the ravine. The second is smaller and nearer the centre, about five feet away from the first. The third encircles the large stones heaped in the form of a low altar where the copperheads crawl to sleep.

Adélard and Philomène are near the altar, the little boy and girl at their feet like altar boys. The guests sit in a circle on the stones.

Munda cor meum, ac labia mea, omnipotens Deus qui labia Isaiae prophetae calculo mundasti ignito.

The Sisters of the Precious Blood piously cross themselves. On the forehead, mouth and heart.

The whisky blanc burns your gullet, hotter than Isaiah's fiery coals. The guests have removed all their clothes and tender their pallid bodies to Philomène's unguent.

"I'm goin' to grease you all up with my drug like little fish in the frying pan."

The high moon shines down into the most secret parts of the ravine, leaving white spots like lime scattered on the ground. Some of the faces are lit by moonbeams: do they know that you cannot with impunity offer your face up to the white sources of the night?

The slow stream of naked bodies advances towards the altar and Philomène's holy, shameless hands. Adélard presents the unguent in a deep dish.

Philomène rubs, massages and greases each hide, young or old, that comes before her. She passes her hands over the entire body with insinuating gentleness which, more pervasive than the unguent itself, penetrates us and releases the captive spirit, making it light and capable of travel beyond the confines of the world.

"You'll hallucinate from head to foot!" assures Philomène, who takes care not to forget the body's finest skin, where it's more sensitive to the drug's penetration: underarms, groin, the hollow behind the knees.

Philomène washes her hands in the basin full of water that the little boy and girl hold out to her.

Never before has Sister Julie been this close to the little girl.

All boundaries have been abolished: I am now rediscovering my childhood. There's no resistance. I match myself to her flesh and bones and warm myself at the source of my lost life, like a cat snuggling by the fire.

Lavabo inter innocentes manus meas et circumdabo altare tuum, Domine.

Let the silent nuns listen to the celebrant! It is I, Sister

Julie, there holding the basin with Joseph, my brother.

Philomène bathes her greasy hands at great length. The surface of the water is streaked with a skin of oily filaments, violet, brown and blue; they float, moving and writhing.

I lift my eyes towards Philomène's moon-white face. I look also at Adélard, aglow with nocturnal light. I believe my parents adore the moon and the moonbeams that pass through them to illuminate the night.

The ground is strewn with heaps of clothes, pitiful or grotesque. Corsets, leather and cloth belts, mottled neckties, women's dresses, men's pants, socks, underpants and brassieres.

Disheveled men and women streaming with sweat and grease now dance around the altar, their faces turned outwards. You can hear a twanging music. A gaunt and haggard adolescent cranks away at an ancient Victrola on his thighs.

The ring loosens, breaks up, is gradually transformed while laughter rises all around. They're dancing two by two, defying the edict of the diocese.

The music becomes strident, more and more out of tune; flattens, sour and harrowing. Cries and wails seem to emanate from the belly of the youth sitting with closed eyelids and tight lips, to mingle with the blues on the phonograph.

Suddenly the music slows down, lowering in pitch, hoarsening, to suffocate completely with a cavernous squeak.

The cortege silently forms to pay homage to Philomène. Now you can hear the crickets shrilling above our heads. In the distance, calls of nocturnal birds of prey.

They've lighted enormous fires of green wood near the piled-up stones. The wind folds the whirling smoke back to the altar where Philomène lies.

Adélard has attached two cow's horns to his forehead and wears a crown of green leaves. He holds a gaily coloured paper parasol over the body of his wife, who is stretched out on her stomach.

The parasol claps shut: everyone freezes, in the expectation of a new world with more excitment and spice than the world of misery and death in which we live.

On the stones, Philomène is moving. She buries her head in her arms. With a movement of her loins, she lifts her rump and tenders it to the homage of her subjects.

Each one passes in turn and kisses Philomène's soft and lightly smoked behind.

Sanctus, sanctus, sanctus
Pleni sunt coeli et terra
Gloria tua,

sing the nuns, skipping over God's name without realizing it, guided by the thin, tiny voice of Sister Julie of the Trinity, somnambulistic but penetrating.

An owl flies in the ravine, above the altar. You can imagine the rustling of his admirable wings. Then he flies off again, straight towards the moon.

The smoke is a cover set over the ravine. Men and women are heavy with visions.

The emaciated student has put another record on the phonograph. He has trouble turning the handle. The adolescent perceives a whirlpool of coloured strings gathering and spreading out in the hollow of his closed hand, which has become transparent like a jellyfish. The sounds become visible even before the needle slips into the first groove of the record. When the music, ripened to a unique perfection, begins to unwind its long sonorous string, tears stream down the boy's face. He is overwhelmed by its genius. His hollow stomach reverberates like a drum, a thousand trumpets and saxes grip and wring his sickly body, confer a hard penis and archangel's hands upon him for the duration of the blues.

Pierrette's gaze is fixed upon the bark of a tree. The

contemplation of this bark is so satisfying, so inexhaustible, that she can't take her eyes off it. The relation between the music and the bark is revealed to her, filling her with joy. Pierrette has been working at the factory since she was fifteen. She stitches leather suitcases. The dust of leather covers her clothes, seeps into her ears, nose, mouth and eyes, all over her white skin. She's never finished washing and scrubbing herself. And now, tonight, at the bottom of the ravine, her foreman's eyes stare at her from the tree. His entire face soon becomes visible around the eyes, is quickly covered with scales of verdigris. The man's mouth shrinks and freezes like a knot of wood drawn on the tree. Terrible threats are uttered in an astonishingly gentle breath.

"Out on the street, Pierrette! Fired! Jobless like everybody else!"

Pierrette watches while the head and body of her boss are gradually and irreparably turned into a tree. Now that he's taken root, the man is completely innocuous, absurd. Pierrette has all eternity before her to make fun of her boss, who's rooted at the bottom of a ravine on the mountain of B . . ., ants nibbling away at his feet and crows' droppings burning his head.

Suddenly Pierrette is laughing. A flight of bells unfurls from her throat. The skinny student cries out that dreams and religion are the opium of the people! He leaves his phono there, on a stone, where its thin voice ripples away. The young man softly walks over the sand towards Pierrette's laugh. Leans over the young girl all smeared with magic unguent. He caresses Pierrette's breasts. And now Pierrette exults from head to foot. The young man lies down on her body.

It's not a question of sinking completely into a sleep stirred by dreams. At this very moment the main event is being played out on the altar smothered in smoke. Philomène is on all fours on top of the pile of stones, like a second altar raised upon the first. Adélard straps the suckling pig bought in the village this morning solidly to Philomène's loins.

The little pig begins screaming at once, as though his death-agony had already begun. The children of darkness stand at the foot of the altar, holding large basins to catch the blood.

Adélard raises his knife high in the air. For a brief instant the blade shines above the father's horned, leafy head. Immense in his complete and hairy nakedness, he has never seemed more terrible nor more majestic. The knife digs into the animal's throat with a muffled sound. Philomène quivers at the shock as though she were about to topple down. It was as if Adélard wanted to sacrifice Philomène along with the piglet.

Philomène holds fast. The screams of the slowly slaughtered beast burst her eardrums. The mother is flooded with warm blood spurting over her back, her face.

Julie trembles. The joy to be seen on her father's face is even more terrifying than the blood spilling into the basin and splashing her fingers. Adélard is radiant with release and satisfaction. His hand firmly holds the knife in the wound. The order of the world is inverted. The most absolute beauty governs this act.

In the audience a man screams. He holds his arm out towards the altar. Swears there is a huge snake there, with a crown on its head — it's about to devour two little black and white rabbits, male and female, who are snuggled against the foot of the altar. (Could it be a grass-snake roused by the fire's warmth?) The man is very excited. He describes what is seen by him alone at length and in great detail. The serpent is devouring his fascinated victims one after the other, according to a well-established plan. First the genitals, then the heart and brain.

A woman laughs: her entire flabby body is gripped by convulsions as if she were weeping. You can barely hear what she says. Something about a large family, about oversized babies borne in frightful pain.

"It's like shitting bricks, ladies and gentlemen."

Suddenly appeased by that confidence, the woman murmurs with an immense gentleness:

"Philomène has promised me to take them out of my belly, the damned little things, when they're still no bigger than an onion and soft as a rosebud."

The woman is sitting on the ground. She spreads her legs. Leans her head over between her flaccid thighs, seems to watch for the coming of a tender series of blossomings promised to Philomène's expert hands.

On the altar Philomène groans, pants, screams in perfect symbiosis with the little pig whose throat has been cut, still attached to her back. The flow of blood diminishes and dries up little by little. The cries become more feeble. One last spasm. Silence falls with death, fills the whole ravine and sweeps into our bones.

Adélard unbinds the animal that's been sacrificed on Philomène's back. His gestures are exceedingly slow and measured.

For a long while Philomène lies on her stomach on the altar, sticky with blood. Dead.

And then she jumps up and rubs her loins and arms. She dips her hands in the basin of blood the children hold out to her, offers a drink to the whole assembly from her two palms and close-pressed fingers.

Hic est enim calix sanguinis mei,
novi et aeterni testamenti
mysterium fidei,

intones the celebrant robed in his green, gold-embroidered chasuble. The white cornets dip in unison, except one among them that remains erect, apparently asleep. The dazzled face of Sister Julie of the Trinity wears a beatific smile beneath her coif.

While Adélard skins, eviscerates and disembowels the suckling pig, to cook it.

Hoc est enim corpus meum.

Now there is great confusion in the convent chapel. The words of the consecration have been inverted.

The freshness of the silence persists and tingles the ends of our fingers. While the phonograph, started up again, slowly unwinds its music in long threads of ice from a spool of snow, despite the warmth of the summer night.

The smoke thickens. The cover is completely drawn over our heads. We are shut up in this ravine in the very intimacy of the earth. A profound experience that we'll no longer have to envy the deceased. Still safe in the privileges of the living, we penetrate the domain of the dead and the sacred places of their refuge. This chill in our veins, this keen smell of earth in our mouths. With astonishing ease, we absorb the night of the dead and their extreme cold, all darkness and terror and horror removed. Raised to higher powers of what we are, we know that life and death hold no more secrets nor torments for us.

The earthen bean pots have been set to cook on buried embers. Sweet corn boils by the potful. While the little suckling pig turns over and over on the spit above the fire, and gleams, and takes on coloured reflections, and loses its fat drop by drop to the bottom of the dripping-pan.

Thanks to Philomène's unguent and the money earned at Georgiana's, the jobless friends had the feast and celebration of their lives that night. They partook of communion in both kinds, paid homage to the sorceress, danced and fornicated until dawn. Adélard and Philomène, their bodies smeared with smoke and dried blood, went from one to the other with savage bounds and piercing cries, waking the sleeping, exciting them, coupling with them, intervening just in time to slip like spectres into the very deepest of dreams already begun.

The children had dozed off near the fire at an early hour, to sleep a natural sleep; they hadn't been rubbed with magical unguent nor drunk any whisky blanc.

The little girl, deep in her first sleep, was roused by someone pushing her with his foot, rather roughly, on the back and legs. A huge shadow of a horned man was standing before her, his face covered with soot, chest rising with heavy breathing. The lower part of his face was hidden by a kind of black, shiny cloth. His distorted and distant voice rang out from behind the mask as though rising from the depths of a cavern.

First the man warned the little girl that he would kill her if she screamed. A knife hung on a string around his neck. The man said he was the devil and he had to possess the little girl. He made her swear never to go to confession at the village church, never to recite any prayer or use holy water. Then he bit her hard on the shoulder to mark her forever as his creature. His skin was slimy, ill-smelling. He took his swollen sex in his hand and forced it into the child's small body. She screamed out in pain. The devil smothered the little girl's cries with his furry hands. And promised, in a barely audible voice, to grant her every wish. She bled a lot; but the devil, upon leaving her, told her it was the blood of the slaughtered pig running down between her thighs, and not her own blood.

At that very moment Sister Julie of the Trinity (having been present all through the sabbat) lifted her veil and identified herself to the devil.

"Do you recognize me, damn you? It's I, Sister Julie, your daughter."

She asked him two favours in the name of the raped child.

1. That Sister Gemma, steeped in her sugary joy, might fall into great disorder and break down in tears once and for all.

2. That the chaplain might reveal, irremediably, his perfect nullity in front of the entire community.

The guests, exhausted, shivering as though plunged into snow, sapped by the visions which released cohorts of angels and monsters in their dreams, collapsed into the wrinkled heaps of their clothes. They slept, transported out of this world, for several days. But you could very well perceive their abandoned bodies if you leaned over the edge of the ravine on the mountain of B. . . .

Ita missa est.

Sister Julie, like most of her companions, is deprived of Holy Communion (the number of hosts having mysteriously diminished on that morning); she feels neither loss nor astonishment. She's punished for having slept during mass, condemned to brush and scrub the long tiled floor leading to the chapel, on her hands and knees.

Sister Gemma, pressed with questions and raked over the coals by Mother Marie-Clotilde, defends herself, cries, insists, and swears by the cross hanging at her neck that she herself counted the hosts before mass, and that there had been enough for the communion of the entire community.

Sister Gemma is demoted from her functions as vestry nun. Mother Marie-Clotilde maintains that her soul has become as dirty as her galoshes during the slushiest weeks of spring.

Sister Gemma is appointed cook.

"You know, cooking is what I like least in the world."

What an incautious declaration, Sister! Blurted out one day at recess with a burst of laughter. You had only to hold your tongue. It didn't fall on deaf ears. Nothing goes unnoticed here. The walls of this convent have elephants' memories. Everything can turn against you when it's time for trial.

A bird's feather in a transparent body. Such was Sister Gemma's soul when she was vestry nun. Nothing seemed to weigh upon her. No chagrin, misery or fault, not even original sin. Sister Gemma enjoyed her innocence with a childish shamelessness. She would stand near the altar and the sacred vessels like a joyous angel. Life was soft and white. Sister Gemma would cut the hosts silently, practically in ecstasy. The long, thin sheets of unleavened bread, a very large host for the priest and smaller ones for the nuns. Sacred signs seemed embroidered in filigree on this extremely white, nearly transparent bread, like the finest paper. When Sister Gemma reflected that our Saviour, body and soul, was going to inhabit the hosts she was cutting, tears of love would come to her eyes. She would think she felt beneath her fingers the pulsing of Christ's blood, spent on the cross for our sins. Sister Gemma would then offer herself up as a victim to the celestial crucified spouse. It would seem to her as though Jesus Christ accepted her offering, piercing her heart with a terrible, gentle blow of the spear.

The sacerdotal garments filled Sister Gemma with fervour and admiration. She used to care for them, wash them, starch them, iron, mend and embroider them and caress them softly, barely brushing them with her hand. As for the browned bones of the blessed father, founder of the convent slain by the Iroquois in 1649, Sister Gemma would often venerate them in the silver reliquary. It would bring a kind of twinge to her heart, as though an angel were warning her in a dream of the fragility of all earthly life. You only have death to cross, Sister. On the other side of the glass, the true, eternal life.

Retired amidst these holy objects, ecstatic in her whiteness and transparency, Sister Gemma had believed she would simply die of love one day, sheltered by the silent sacristy and steeped in the odour of candles and incense, and be forever delivered up from all profane contact.

And now she finds herself in the kitchen, where she's assailed by all that dirties, smears, splashes, runs over, skins, cuts and burns. The livid hands of the vestry nun flounder in meat and blood, giblets, fish scales, chicken feathers. She makes blunder after blunder, reaps rebuke after rebuke, punishment after punishment. She sniffles more and more often, sheds tears in her large men's handkerchief, vomits secretly.

Sister Julie is behind Sister Gemma, watching and waiting. The slightest failure, the smallest tear are keenly apprehended, impatiently desired.

Trencher, knife, hatchet, bone saw. Sister Gemma is bent over her butcher's stall. She contrives to cut up an enormous quarter of beef set on the wooden block. Her white cuffs are stained with blood.

"All this sickens me! If I didn't know there was a hereafter, I'd close shop this very minute!"

"Remember the three young men in the furnace. They praised the Lord, if I remember right? And the saintly Job on his dung pile?"

The knife falls from Sister Gemma's hands and plants itself upright in the kitchen linoleum. She kneels amidst her scattered skirts, tries to disengage the knife. Rises, knife in hand. She faces Sister Julie.

"A knife planted in the floor, sign of company, Sister. Here I am. I'm your company. I've arrived."

"You're always on my back, Sister Julie. Leave me alone, I beg you. Anybody would think you wanted to get me down."

Sister Julie pushes Sister Gemma away from the table. She cuts and slices the piece of meat. Her gestures are sure and precise, light and joyous.

Sister Gemma will later be heard to say that her hands seemed to be flying over the table.

Benedicite, Domine . . .

Heads are lowered and raised. Hands trace the sign of the cross, over and over again.

Sounds of life burst out for one brief instant, to be stifled at birth. Long benches with no backs that you pull out from under the table. Tired bodies crowded in upon them. Stirring of dishes and silverware.

Silence.

From the height of her tribune the reader begins *recto tono*.

Sister Gemma rushes in from the kitchen and begs pardon for her lateness. She rolls her sleeves down, wipes her forehead, proceeds to her place.

"Dear God, don't let me have the chipped cup, or I'll believe you've sent me a sign of rejection."

We are shut up in a world of forebodings and omens. You have your sign, Sister. For the third time in a row.

Look well, there, to the right of your plate. The thick white crockery cup, easily recognized among all others, with distinct grey chips all around? And that crack hanging from top to bottom, thin as a hair? But then you shouldn't have provoked God. His silence is sometimes preferable to His word. So listen to that implacable word.

On the other side of the table, directly opposite, Sister Julie studies Sister Gemma's gentle face carefully, on the watch for the first signs of despair.

Sister Gemma puts the flat of her hand on the table to ask for bread, Sister Julie hands her the bread basket immediately. Sister Gemma forms a circle with her thumb and index, Sister Julie quickly serves her water.

Express yourself by gestures. Such is the rule in the refectory. Don't touch the silence, or as little as possible. Deaf mutes have a more complex vocabulary than ours. Hope eventually to attain the absolute non-word, strive for that perfection.

The tiniest things take on an extravagant importance. Nothing is discarded. Nothing is lost. (Don't we go to the point of collecting the greasy swill of the dishwater to make soap of it?) Nothing gets lost here, except one's reason.

You'll have to account to God for the slightest bit of thread wasted, for a worn shoe put aside before it's completely unusable, for a cake of soap thrown out before it becomes as transparent as a drop of water. At least you don't have to decide anything yourself. Your will is no longer yours. The vow of obedience dispenses you of all decisions, all initiative.

If you don't become like little children, little tiny children at the breast, you won't enter into the kingdom of heaven. Blind obedience, innocent laughter, gentle foolishness, the enormous chagrin of scolded children, the daily pinpricks, the knife blows dealt to the heart; all of it drowned in an incomparable silence. The bottom of the ocean rediscovered. Mother house. Womb-house. Life comes here to expire in long muted waves against the stone stairs.

Some news filters in all the same, on parlour days. They talk about the war going on over there in the old countries. France is occupied. England is bombed. A brother, a cousin have been carried off by a foreign death in a foreign land, for a foreign war. There was a terrible story of Carmelites raped by communists that upset the whole community. But that was in Spain, and several years have since gone by.

At night, phantoms crawl over the garden wall and pass through the heavy, double-locked doors. The Paraclete impregnates us in turn. The fruit of our wombs is blessed.

The Angel of the Lord declared unto Mary
And she conceived of the Holy Ghost
And the Word was made flesh
And dwelt among us.

In our dreams, adorable Christ-children nestle in our arms. Sometimes the Holy Ghost appears to us, masked and costumed, often unrecognizable and troubling; he looks like the butcher's boy or the piano tuner, or even like Monseigneur himself.

Fathers and mothers also visit us at night. No longer shy and intimidated with the real little worn-dime faces they wear in the parlour, but transfigured, blazing with anger or beaming with love, concise and authoritative. In the form of a brown bear. Or in the guise of a sacred cow. Or reduced to a cloud of dazzling snow.

We're haunted, my Sisters. Through the white cell-curtains drawn for the night seeps a vague murmur of sleepers breathing. The nightlight throws a pale glow on the polished wooden passage. Eyeballs moving beneath closed eyelids. Images passing by.

In nomine Patris.

A woman's voice rises, veiled at first then clearer and sharper, almost a scream, announcing the victory of light over darkness. Responses befogged with sleep rise up here and there behind the closed curtains of the cells.

O Jesus, through the Immaculate Heart of Mary, I offer Thee all my prayers, works, joys and sufferings of this day, in union with the Holy Sacrifice of the Mass throughout the world, in reparation for my sins and for all the intentions of Thy Sacred Heart. . . .

Three Sundays in a row the laugh of Sister Julie of the Trinity resounded in the chapel during Father Migneault's sermon.

On the third Sunday Father Migneault didn't finish his sermon. He left the pulpit hastily. Mocked in his very core, reduced to the strict truth — ridiculous preacher and very ordinary man, chaplain of a very ordinary convent — Father Migneault saw himself for what he really was. And that view was intolerable. He never dared to write another sermon.

He came to fear meeting Sister Julie. He never quite succeeded in lowering his eyes before the yellow mocking glance reached him at a turn of the corridor. Sister Julie's destructive power was at work on the chaplain, and it met no resistance there. It was imperative that the man be cast down, that he recognize his total insignificance. Sister Julie was absolutely sure of it, like one who has received a mission. Cast down — Father Migneault would be cast down.

Sister Julie forgot to pray for her brother off at the war.

The chaplain began to suffer from insomnia, nocturnal sweating and nightmares. Gnawed by insects, crushed by iron and steel machines, torn to pieces, mashed to crumbs, called a failure by his father and a good-for-nothing by his mother (both of them had crocodile's jaws and scales), he finally gave in to the fact: his perfect nonentity in this world. And so strong was his desire to confess this to Sister Julie, to be absolved of being such a nothing (she alone had that power), that he summoned her to his office. Threw himself down at her feet, clasped her knees in his hands, buried his head in the wide folds of her black skirt and cried like a child, dispossessed of his very life.

Sister Julie was governed by an absolute necessity far stronger than herself: while her rough hands caressed the chaplain's tonsured head, her soft, almost gentle voice informed him that she could do nothing for him.

"You're just a little fool. You've never been anything but a little fool."

Father Migneault left the convent of the ladies of the Precious Blood that very evening, never to return.

Sister Julie received her punishment for having laughed in the chapel: she was to wear the spiked bracelet well hidden under her sleeve every Friday of the month, in remembrance of the Passion of our Saviour.

I, Marie-Clotilde of the Cross, Superior of this convent, myself dependant upon our Superior General who is responsible to our Mother Provincial, herself subject to our Mother General in Rome; all women, every one, never priests, but victims on the altar with Christ, led, advised and directed by our superiors general, bishops and cardinals all the way up to the supreme chief and certified male under his white robes, His Holiness the Pope: I swear and declare that all is in order in this house.

We are a contemplative order, lay sister and choir sister in turn, without caste or privilege. Our tasks are allotted according to the mysterious necessities of salvation and the orderly running of the house.

Each nun does her utmost to practise the vow of poverty in the destitution of her daily life. But once united in council, sitting opposite the notary and the lawyer, the Mother Superior, the Mother Assistant and the Mother Bursar give themselves over body and soul to the financial game. Initial shares. Dividends. Capital. Buying and Selling. Land in the country. Houses in the upper and lower town. The sisters are formidable in council; they face their adversaries without batting an eyelash. The starched white of the cornets and wimples, the black lustreless material of the robes, pale hands and drawn faces. All this established for eternity. A live nun quickly takes the place of the dead nun who has just been buried, apparently without the adversary's even taking notice of the substitution. The sisters of the council bear a perfect likeness to each other. A row of little birds of prey, hieratic and indestructible. The ruthless passion of profits. The absolute certainty of one's rights. The clear conscience that makes one merciless.

In the wash-house.

"For an hour's labour, an eternity of bliss."

Edifying thought posted on the wash-house wall, in the vapour rising from the steaming tubs and boilers. Soap, scrub, rinse and wring. All the month's linen, large and small, to be done. The nuns bend over the tubs and scrub without speaking, with a bubbling of water and rubbing of washboards.

Sister Gemma furtively unrolls her blood-stained menstrual cloths in the soapy water while her companions look on impassively.

Sister Julie thinks that she really should wash her nightgown. Will I have enough humility to ask the permission of our Mother Superior once again? She's already turned me down twice to punish me. And why bother about a nightgown anyway? The more I steep in my filth, the easier it is to escape from the convent, the greater the compliments I earn elsewhere: I'm all the more content and joyous in another world.

Is it because of the stifling hot wash-house vapour that is so like the fog banks so often seen in the mountain hollow? Once again the mysterious space of the mountain of B . . . opens up to receive Sister Julie of the Trinity. A white downy vapour. Shortly afterwards you can see the ground where you have to put your feet. You definitely feel that you're mounting a steep rise. Grey sand. Rolling pebbles. The little path leads up to the shanty. The fog unravels and dissipates completely.

Philomène is sitting on the steps in front of the door. Midday. Her yellow hair rolled up in curlers. Her pink dress torn under the arms, her black moist armpits.

She holds her arms out to the little girl who comes running, tousled and lousy, smeared with blackberries.

"My little piggy, my little slut, my darling little turdlet, my very own nummy-child."

The mother's wondrous words. Her wondrous odour. The little girl snuggles up in the maternal lap. The marvellous pink dress, already faded and dirty, its tiny purple flowers half faded. Underneath, big, soft, comfortable thighs. Bliss.

Harsh midday bursting out all around, yellow and green, shrill. The Angelus ringing softly in the distance, down by the village. Adélard is standing in the summer sun. Greenish-black suit and matching felt hat, white shirt, black pointed shoes, black tie, bloody lips, red beard. His arms filled with grass for the rabbits. His eyes blink in the light. He looks at Philomène holding her daughter on her knees. Adélard desires his wife and his daughter with an equal and violent longing, both bound together, one and the same flesh of which he'd be the absolute master.

But he shoos the child away.

"Scat, little Flea. Hurry up."

Adélard throws down his armful of grass on the sand.

Philomène has taken her dress off. She lies on the rabbits' grass and gives out lively little yelps to call Adélard.

The little girl goes off towards the woods. She hears Adélard answering Philomène's call with a muted clamour, like the cry of a lumberjack about to fell a tree. Then resounding smacks on rounded buttocks.

The little girl joins the little boy, who is squatting in the brambles stuffing himself with handfuls of wild blackberries. The little girl also kneels down, picks and eats all the red and black berries within reach. Having gone round the bush methodically stripping it, the children come back together, shoulder to shoulder, knee to knee. They smear themselves with blackberries, all over their faces, arms and legs, lick each other in the moist heat of the brush at noon.

Sister Julie, erect in the wash-house vapour, sleeps on. Her breathing is long and deep. Perfectly blissful, Sister Julie leans on nothing. All the nuns have stopped working to watch Sister Julie sleep. The sight is so moving that no one thinks of waking her. But at one point Sister Léonard pulls Sister Julie by the arm to move her away from the tub, fearing she might fall into it. Sister Julie's arm stays up and away from her body, exactly as Sister Léonard left it. Sister Léonard pulls Sister Julie's other arm hard behind her, and the arm stays there, stiff and unmoving. Now all the little nuns file before Sister Julie. To see who'll bend her head toward one shoulder or move her feet on the wet tiles, as though they'd been given a mechanical doll.

Sister Julie sleeps on. Sister Gemma alone refuses to touch Sister Julie in such a strange state. She's terrified. Soon Sister Julie's vague smile changes into irresistible, uncontrollable laughter. She's shaken from head to toe by a storm of pleasure, as though she were being tickled. But she doesn't wake up. She sticks her tongue out as if eating an ice cream cone. Her belly and rump shake frenetically, in a quite indecent fashion.

Mother Marie-Clotilde has been alerted: with a shaking voice she declares that it's undoubtedly a case of St.

Vitus's dance coupled with an attack of somnambulism.

Sister Julie, slapped and splashed with ice-cold water, regains consciousness. She falls to her knees on the wet tiles at her Superior's feet, begs her in a thin, hypocritical voice to have pity on her and pardon her sins.

Mother Marie-Clotilde (even if she doesn't have the right, the priest alone . . .) is strongly tempted to pardon the unknown sins that Sister Julie claims to have committed in a dream, just to restore peace as quickly as possible among her daughters. They've been changed into statues of salt, their sleeves rolled up to the elbow, their hands red and soapy, their feet stuck in puddles, their eyes round and mouths gaping, their very souls exposed to every wind that blows.

Just then Sister Julie lifts her head. Fleeting as a slash of lightning, her glance strikes the Superior; it is furtive, absolutely animal and elusive. Sister Julie's yellow eye quickly disappears beneath her wide eyelid while the blind face keeps on beaming with an impudent joy.

Of course Mother Marie-Clotilde takes care not to consult the community's doctor about Sister Julie's case. She awaits an event that's already been secretly set in motion, and doesn't want to undertake anything that might hinder it. She strongly desires and accepts this secret event in the blackest part of her soul. Shivers run up her spine as though she had a fever. She is completely given over to her waiting. As are the girls that have been confided to her. Only the absence of God can explain this, this lack, this tangible anxiety that pervades the convent.

The mirthful face, cropped by the coif, shines softly. Then Sister Julie's lips start moving as if she were reciting her beads to herself. The Superior, intrigued, bends over. A very vulgar little sentence can be read on Sister Julie's lips. The Superior starts, and blushes to the very roots of her hair.

"My own joyous mysteries, Mother, you can always stuff them up somewhere!"

Night, like a slack, bottomless, gleamless sea. A locked cell, like a closed fist. On the white wall a black cross, a silver Christ. The Superior can't get to sleep. Sitting on the edge of her bed, glasses put aside, swaddled for sleep like a bolt of cloth, she lets her big naked feet and knotty ankles hang over the edge. Her big eyes, like those of a frightened mare, roll from right to left and from left to right. The Superior of the Sisters of the Precious Blood has just rediscovered, intact, the very first terror of her far-off childhood: the almost total certainty that the devil is hiding under the bed and that any minute now he's going to pull her down by the feet and gobble her up.

There are thirteen of us at table today, notes the Superior. She crosses herself with a quick rap of the thumb on her breast.

An ancient nun has escaped from the infirmary to which she's been confined for years. She sits down just beside Sister Julie, attracted by Sister Julie, needing Sister Julie, waiting for an order from Sister Julie. She asks for bread and water, still remembering the prescribed gestures, though very slow and trembling. Brown spots on aged hands. Folds of skin on the yellow face, glued to shrunken bones. The mummified little body tightly bound in the wrappings of death. The choking heart.

The old nun lifts her eyes towards Sister Julie, a question in her gaze. And Sister Julie smiles at the elderly Sister: she'd been waiting only for this sign of assent to die in peace. She collapses on the floor, her knees bent up to her chin, her hands between her thighs, shrivelled up:

instantly breakable like glass.

They found a crumpled piece of paper on the infirmary floor near the undone bed. A testament. Big, shapeless, child-like letters all awry, almost illegible.

"I'm too old. I'm fed up with living. I've neither the strength nor the rope to hang myself. Thank you, sweet Jesus."

SISTER AMELIE OF THE AGONY

It had been easy for Sister Julie to answer Sister Amélie's call and fulfil her desire.

It's on the mountain of B . . . that Sister Julie obtains all kinds of favours and renews her strength and her powers.

The red-headed man lies down on top of me. He claims to be the devil, but I believe he's my father. My father is the devil.

He no longer threatens to kill me if I scream. He lets me scream because there's no one in the shanty now, no one nearby. Besides, my screaming pleases him.

No light in the shanty now, no lamps or candles. Night everywhere. The room is as small as a box. Perhaps it's a fir coffin? The odour of mildewed wood and moist night — I think I'll never be rid of it.

This time the hole he digs in me is so deep that all the beasts of the forest will be able to dive into it as into a burrow.

Philomène doesn't stop to remove her blue hat with the golden bird and red rose. She dresses her daughter's wounds and chides her. She laughs.

"And I told you to watch out. Men will be men. I can't

even take a little trip to Georgiana's, to the city, but . . . Don't bawl, my little slut. You really had a going-over. There, you won't feel the worse for it on your wedding day. Drink this."

Philomène's special tea steams in a large red cup that I've never seen before. I'm lying on the kitchen table, my belly wadded with cotton, like a dead bird that's just been stuffed. Philomène lifts my head with her hands to make me drink. A taste of bitter bark sticks to my teeth, grips my palate and makes me want to vomit.

"Sleep. You're a big girl now. You'll give birth to a toad if you're not careful. Sleep, my lovely."

She's still holding my head in her hands, on her knees. She strokes my hair.

Never again will I be able to sleep, or even shut my eyes. I turn my face to the wall. The light mark of the blue hat Philomène hasn't put back in place against the darkened boards. A large circle like a flat plate, a rusty nail in its centre. I have only to fix my eyes on the pale disc and the point in its middle with all my might to keep from dozing off.

My entire will strains to see, while around me familiar objects become more and more distorted and take on fantastic aspects as Philomène's drink takes effect inside me.

The white moon on the wall (the place where Philomène usually hangs her blue hat) assumes the width and reassuring thickness of the mother's powerful belly. The bellybutton like a small motionless eye. The black fuzzy pubis.

Someone says you must look the night straight in the eye; if you blink just once all is lost. To see, at the risk of death, the chance to live twice.

Philomène makes herself up carefully. Violet areolas, red nipples, beautiful enormous blue breasts. All over her body minute marks in a rainfall of colours.

Adélard stands before Philomène. She attaches the horns and crown of leaves on his head. His long thin body is smeared black. His ribs carefully drawn in red. He doesn't look the least bit piteous. On the contrary. An infinite pride beams from his every pore. His glory comes from the wrong he's done me. His glory reflects upon me, at the center of my slashed belly. His glory suddenly invades me like a raging light. I want to turn cartwheels in the sun, legs spread so that everyone can see my wound and honour me for it. Let the atrocious be changed into good. Such is the law: the world wrong side up.

From now on all powers and privileges are mine. Having suffered, I demand to be honoured. Having partaken of my father's shame, I desire to be crowned with fire and iron, with and by him.

"Queen and martyr, Sister Julie of the Trinity, pray for us."

"No man may look upon the devil, but must die."

These words are pronounced by a bodiless, soulless voice, somewhere in the shanty. I can see the orange colour of it as it passes before my eyes. I seize all it says. I know as much as Satan himself, but I am not yet aware of what I know.

Adélard has stuck a piece of black material on his face again. Sometimes that man is my father. He talks to me with his face uncovered. Says very ordinary things. He says "sure is freezin' out", or "the air's real warm this mornin'."

Philomène still holds my head on her knees. She's using words that are strange to me. Talking about a girl turned woman and the initiation that must follow its course.

I lie naked on my back on the kitchen table, my head on my mother's knees.

A circle has been drawn with white chalk on the floor, all around the table. The few faithful who have been granted entry to the shanty stand perfectly still on the edge of the circle, concentrating on the drunkenness rising up in them, awaiting the promised ceremony. They fix me with widened eyes. Consenting and given over, I'll be the core of their ecstasy. Adélard and Philomène have promised that. It must be so. They'll glorify me as an equal to my father and mother. Inside and outside the planked shanty. Over the entire mountain of spruce and birch trees, where the wind of malediction blows on stormy evenings.

It's a closed room. The rough wooden door carefully shut. The new knife-hewn latch becomes more and more clearly outlined against the darkened boards. The greyish shutters have been nailed down over the windows. I see the red and yellow daylight through the cracks. It's fall. I'm cold. The ancient oilcloth clings to my shoulder blades.

The spectators undress. Their clothes fall to the floor where they remain to be tread in measure under naked feet, mechanically, as if the spirit were elsewhere. Rhythmic padding of feet on the crumpled clothing. A kind of closed-mouth chant begins to rise then, coming from the back of the throat, hoarse sighs.

Philomène makes me take large gulps from the red cup. The sound of my blood running down between my thighs, leaving me with a soft singing complaint, delights me. Philomène says horrible things to me: they seem so soft and tender I could die. I understand the converse of my mother's ferocious words. I see the words coming out of her mouth. They fly out like soap bubbles to rise toward the blackened beams of the ceiling and break with a light plop.

Philomène assures me that I must be drained of all my blood, bled white like a chicken. The blood of childhood is rotten and must disappear to be replaced by the magic semen.

Murmurs in the assembly: they begin singing louder, faster, with violence, clapping their hands, their whole bodies writhing.

Now I am on all fours on the table, lying on my stomach, looking like my mother on the altar at the bottom of the ravine the other summer. They place a little board on the small of my back and on it a tiny black square stove, already alight and burning. They say it's to cook the unleavened bread.

No weight on my back, no burning sensation. I am light and soft, obedient and ravished, my mother's equal, my father's spouse. My peace has no equal but my pride. I'm busy following on the floor the luminous paths of the incantations that rise up towards me with a gasping, breathless rhythm. Unknown words become visible, have funny, malicious, raving colours that are often outrageous to the eye, like firebrands. I suppose they are blasphemy: filth and mortal wounds they throw on me to ease their hearts. I seize an entire sentence that makes me laugh.

"Cow, cow, young cow on all fours, hear our prayer."

My senses will soon be so fine that I'll apprehend at the first try a man's open heart through the thickness of his clothes and flesh. I'll hear his deepest cry in its first language. I'll extract his most secret desire from between his ribs. That's the way it was for Sister Amélie of the Agony, whom death had forgotten in her bed: didn't I make her descend the long stairway and three stories to let her spend her last puff of breath? The old grateful nun dead at my feet, her last prayer answered. Amen.

"Sister Julie of the Trinity, daughter of rape and incest, hear us, hear our prayer."

Time is long in the hermetically closed shanty. The air thickens into a black smoke. Tension rises. The noise becomes intolerable. A woman leans against the wall to keep herself from falling, screams that she can bear no more, that she wants to leave. They slap her and get her drunk.

The young girl lying flat on her stomach on the table begins to whimper. She quivers under the weight of the fire that burns her. Philomène laughs.

"It's just what you need, my daughter. It's your burn that must cook the bread, just as if you were a real lighted stove."

The girl lifts her head to look at her mother's face leaning over her. Philomène's grating laugh is distorted like a reflection at the bottom of a battered and dirty cauldron.

"Hideous." My mother's face is "hideous", thinks the girl who's never heard this word — yet she sees it written on her mother's face. Life is no longer anything but nightmares and visions. For an instant the word "hideous" flies up from Philomène's face, a yellowish spot with a sulphurous odour, hides itself behind a beam on the ceiling to lie in wait.

"Hideous. Hideous. Hideous." I'll force the evil out of each one's body. I'll confess them all. I'll deliver them of their sins. So with the horror in my mother's face. At this very moment my power defines itself and melts, while the fire, like a beast all claws out, clutches at my loins. Myself the fire and fire's food, I'm the host of our strange communion.

"May her blood be on us and on our children!"

"May her tears be on us and on our children!"

They take communion in the two kinds. Bread and blood, in an indescribable din. A few fall to the ground and stay there with turned-up eyes. The father and mother offer their daughter to be eaten and drunk.

A crown on my head, the crimson cloak on my shoulders, hands and feet bound, Philomène and Adélard lift me up in their arms and take me around the chalk circle, calling upon the Powers of Darkness and the Gods of the North, East, South and West in a hoarse, low voice. They offer up their burned and consecrated daughter. The wind begins to whistle around the shanty. Enormous whips snap at our house in the night. Philomène dresses my wounds and looks after me once again. She makes me drink. I've sworn to obey in everything.

I fall asleep rolled up in a blanket on the table. Around me, the uneasy breathing of the sleepers frees terrible or radiant dreams that flit about the room like fireflies that dim and die out one by one.

Deep in sleep I see an immense tree covered with tempting red and black fruit like enormous blackberries. Philomène's voice, metamorphosed, professorial, pedantic, comes softly, close to my ear.

"It's the tree of knowledge, the tree of life, the serpent that vanquished God — it's now been planted in your body, my little turdlet. You're my daughter and you carry on my tradition. Your father the devil has begot you a second time."

I think I slept three straight days and nights.

I'm wakened by a salty freshness on my cheeks. I see my brother looking at me. He's crying. My brother's pity bathes my face in tears. I also cry.

"Julie, Julie, my poor Julie."

"Where were you, Joseph? Where were you?"

"In the woods. I don't stay around when them folks are in the house."

Once again my heart beats as it used to. Ordinary life is still possible. Joseph says he's caught a two-pound bass, he's going to cook it for me.

Just time to eat the fish grilled on a fire of twigs and throw the bones away; the autumn twilight is already upon us. The big black pines, near the earth- and straw-coloured shanty with its blind windows, seem to harbour a greyish nest that's been abandoned, fallen just there, exposed to all the dangers of stalking death.

Joseph tells me he knows safe hiding places in the woods and that we must get away from here as fast as we can.

Penetrated with my superiority and importance, I confess to him that I've been initiated, that I can no longer leave. My strange pride.

The poignant odour of autumn all around us.

Prayer leads to everything, if you can come out of it unscathed. To go back and forth freely from the convent to the mountain of B . . ., from the mountain of B . . . to the convent. To commute in time, between the thirties and forties. The trip grows ever easier for Sister Julie. No one even suspects that she accomplishes it on her knees in the chapel among her companions during the hour of daily meditation.

But this morning Sister Julie — her pious tranquillity and total attention to her prayers haven't gone unnoticed — faints and falls full length, half lying on her pew, her legs caught under the prie-dieu. Her skirts stained with blood.

The doctor they've called talks of a possible fibroma in the womb. He doesn't dare prescribe an examination because of the hemorrhage. He prescribes complete rest. Upon discovering the burn in the small of Sister Julie's back, suspecting some insane religious mortification, he rudely questions her on its cause.

Sister Julie doesn't answer. She seems to hear nothing. Like a creature in a coma. Two devouring eyes set in a pallid face fixed upon the doctor. He musters all his will power to keep from lowering his eyes. But he senses that he is *seen*, penetrated to the bone as though being sucked in, chewed and spit out again with disgust on the brightly waxed floor, like a spoonful of porridge.

Several minutes go by. Doctor Painchaud makes it a point of honour not to be the first to look away.

Suddenly Sister Julie turns her head to the wall and starts to cry.

The doctor leaves the convent, conscious of having escaped from great danger. He promises himself to operate on Sister Julie, to remove "all that stuff" that sours her body and soul. *Convent sickness* — he'd read about it somewhere. Keep her from doing harm, render her powerless, shut her dirty yellow eyes for the duration of a good anaesthesia; hold her life and death in my hands, open her belly and sew it back up at will, throw in the garbage all this obscene paraphernalia (ovaries and womb), serving no earthly purpose.

He delights in his fury. He's usually so very gentle and compassionate, he doesn't recognize himself. Can a man suddenly turn himself inside out like a glove and perceive in a flash his deformed double as if in a distorting mirror?

Sister Julie's cat's eye, her owl's eye extracted from its socket, placed in Jean Painchaud's hand. For non-professional use. No dissection or medical use possible. An apparently anodyne stone, conceived, in fact, for reflecting the best concealed of hearts.

Thus the doctor of the ladies of the Precious Blood, a chaste and sensible old bachelor, falls asleep. Delirious.

Far into his deepest sleep, he feels exceedingly short of breath. An enormous weight crushes his chest. He can hear his heart beating. He must take his pulse — he tries to shift his right hand towards his left wrist, but he cannot make the slightest movement. Sweat runs down his forehead into his eyes, and he can do nothing to wipe it.

Sister Julie is sitting heavily on his chest, straddling him with her back turned. The burn sparkles at her loins. She becomes heavier and heavier. An impassive block of stone. A millstone.

"I'm going to die of suffocation," the doctor thinks.

Sister Julie's flat, bland voice is heard somewhere in the room, separated from Sister Julie's body, seemingly coming from the green velvet curtain at the window.

"Count on me, darling treasure of pious souls, doctor of my heart, I'll pull the swinishness out of you through every pore of your dirty body, close-shaved and bathed in holy water."

Sister Julie's weight is more and more oppressing. While voluptuousness rises up in waves, carries the doctor beyond the death he fears and desires.

Sister Julie's voice hovers over him now, like an invisible bird.

"I'm your night-mère, your night-witch. Don't you recognize me? I'm taking you with me. To see a little countryside. And I'll ride you to death, my poor wee idiot horse."

The doctor finally utters a cry. He sits up on the sofa that serves as a bed. Trembling like a leaf. He lights the lamp, finds himself alone in his office. The window is open. The green velvet curtain flapping in the wind.

The doctor is exhausted, but he changes his pyjamas and sheets, anxious to erase all compromising traces of the night, before the cleaning woman comes.

Though Mother Marie-Clotilde, who accompanied Doctor Painchaud, was the only one to have seen, seen with her own eyes, the second-degree burn on Sister Julie's lower back, the astonishing news nevertheless spreads through the entire convent. Whispers, mouth pressed to ear. Some even murmur that Sister Julie, streaming with blood, received the stigmata of Our Lord during morning meditation.

The very next morning the blisters had already disappeared as they had come; and Sister Julie, pressed with questions, cannot explain their origin. The hemorrhage has completely subsided, and the little nun immediately requests permission to take up her convent life again. But she begs the Superior to dispense her from morning devotions for a while, pleading great fatigue.

Sister Julie's humble and submissive look worries Marie-Clotilde. She quickly grants the requested dispensation. Overcoming her disgust and fear, she examines Sister Julie while the nursing sister looks on. A smooth and pearly-white scar shines softly at the small of Sister Julie's back.

The nurse points out to the Superior that Sister Julie also has another very clear mark, on her right shoulder, as if she'd been bitten.

Beginning of Holy Week. Order seems to have been restored. Each morning Sister Julie peels vegetables in the kitchen instead of going to prayer. As for the doctor, he hasn't set foot in the convent, merely enquiring after his patient by telephone. He promises to stop by the convent after Easter vacation.

Mother Marie-Clotilde remains convinced that the spirit of evil has entered her house. She doesn't know how to chase it out again (or rather doesn't dare), seeks Sister Julie's file to no avail among the well-organized convent records. The Superior becomes desperately agitated, flies up and down stairs imposing punishments and penances without rhyme or reason, suppresses all sedatives in the infirmary, as though trying to associate the sick, the senile, the mad, and the possessed with her task of saving the house from this great peril.

Mother Marie-Clotilde endangers her own health by outrageous fasting and endless prayers that leave her faint, on the brink of tears. She writes to the Mother Provincial and to the archdiocese, begging for help and a new chaplain, but in vain.

No answer. The outside world remains silent. The convent is seemingly forsaken by man and God.

The Superior turns to the Mother Assistant and the Mother Bursar. United in council, the three nuns discuss in hushed tones Sister Julie of the Trinity's case. They decide to part with Sister Julie as soon as possible, before it's too late, and draw up a long report for the archdiocese.

It begins in the infirmary, that cloister of cloisters, where all the Sisters of the Precious Blood, normally dispersed in about fifteen convents across the country, come to die. Such is the Rule. The Alma Mater must gather up those who are fit for no more than to suffer and pass on.

What a mistake, Reverend Mother. You should never have deprived the ill and suffering of their sedatives. You have only unleashed weeping and gnashing of teeth, curses and blasphemy, stark brutal pain and naked horror. *In pace*. The secret of despair was well guarded. No death, however strange, was ever called a suicide. No love between nuns, heart-rending as it might be, was ever called love. No burning caress, however fleeting and tender, was ever called a caress.

Sister John of the Cross, immense, rises from her crib, staggers on her big feet. Eighty years old, a catheter permanently placed in her bladder, a plastic bag full of urine attached to her thigh. She calls out for little Sister Jérémie of the Holy Face who would always smile stealthily at her as she held out the holy water after mass. Sixty years ago.

Sister Agathe hums a barrack-room song that her brothers taught her at least fifty years ago. She says it's to put the little Christ-child to sleep in her arms — he just won't stop bawling and drooling.

Sister Lucie of the Angels treads upstairs and down with an unsteady gait. She knocks on all the doors, asking at each one, in a creaky voice, if this is really her parents' house: 92 rue Saint Augustin.

Sister Sophie, covered all over with purulent sores, repeats breathlessly "Thy will be done" and "God have pity on me." Sometimes, after a particularly long wail, she adds, "Pardon, Lord, I beseech Thy pardon for my sins and those of the whole world."

Sister Angèle is twenty. She cries softly, almost tenderly, in a throbbing nasal voice. Never stopping: "I don't want to die, not yet, not now. I implore you, sweet blessed Virgin."

But the cry of Sister Constance of the Peace is without a doubt the most unbearable: blind and half-paralysed, she lets out hoarse, inhuman groans that go on till morning, rhythmic, jerky, as though struck on an anvil: "My God, why hast Thou forsaken me? Why? Why? O God, where art Thou? Where art Thou?"

This infernal racket floods the convent, keeping awake all the healthy ones, those of us who stifle our dreams and phantasms like sins. The nuns in the infirmary, closest to death and birth, don't fall silent until morning and then they fall asleep like little children torn to pieces by stray dogs.

You really shouldn't have done that, Mother Marie-Clotilde. You shouldn't have. What demon inspired you, Mother? (It can only be a demon.) You shouldn't have taken the sedatives away from the infirmary. See what it has brought you to: you ask yourself for the first time, from the bottom of your heart, of what use human suffering? What barbarian God, himself victim and accomplice, nailed to the cross, dares to proclaim that suffering is precious as gold, good as bread, and that it alone can save the world, wrench it from the forces of evil and deliver it from the clutches of sin? Eternal salvation. Its exorbitant price. All that is a scandal, Mother!

What state have you got yourself into, Mother? Into what dark abyss have you now thrust yourself? The sin against the Holy Ghost, maybe that's what it is, this doubt, this new calling in question of God's order, this despondency of your whole being, steeped in darkness? Human pain: all that is left visible in the night, like an intolerably bright star.

Mother Marie-Clotilde does an act of contrition while waiting to go to confession. The new chaplain is due to arrive the next day.

She orders that the doses of sedatives prescribed for all the infirmary patients be doubled. The entire convent then seems plunged into complete torpor night and day. Because Holy Week has already begun, bringing with it strict compulsory silence.

Sister Julie stoops over the kitchen sink peeling cabbages and carrots. With weightless, slow-motion movements, like those made underwater. But she suddenly quickens, and begins avidly reading news of the war on the paper the vegetables are wrapped in.

Commando units raided the region of Dieppe in occupied France early this morning. One-third of the forces engaged in the battle consists of Canadian soldiers.

Sister Julie hasn't had any news of her brother for such a long time. What if he were fighting in Dieppe? What if he had already met with misfortune? Could it be that Sister Julie is responsible (because of her bad behaviour in the convent) for her brother's death? It's not really worth being clairvoyant if you can find out nothing about what means more to you than anything else in the world. Sister

Julie bites her fists with vexation. If only Joseph isn't at Dieppe! How to find out? How to ward off fate?

She promises herself to observe faithfully all the Holy Week exercises in order to keep her brother from harm.

May the catastrophe lurking near Joseph be driven off forever! May my hands joined in prayer protect him against bullets and shrapnel. Pray constantly. Mortify myself without pity.

Sister Gemma claims Sister Julie uttered a loud cry and abruptly pulled her hands from beneath the cold running water in which she was washing vegetables.

All week long Sister Julie wore blisters on her two palms, as though she had been scalded through a sieve. Until Easter Sunday (the day she received Joseph's letter). She continued peeling and washing vegetables each morning and joining her hands to pray during the interminable Easter week ceremonies, desiring with her whole heart to do penance, in union with the Passion of Our Lord.

The *missa tenebrae*.

Three days. Three nocturns.

Worn out by fasting and penance, veils turned down over their faces, personal identity obliterated, turned into statues under the violet drapes, the nuns must descend to hell. They must touch and denounce the very depths of their souls and sins. Grasp and confirm their deepest love and suffering. The flickering flame of joy must be kept low until Easter morning.

The first night reminds us of the treason plotted in darkness, and the agony of Gethsemane.

The second night evokes Christ's death in the darkness of Calvary.

The third night we keep watch over the tomb.

Three times, fifteen candles are lit on the great triangular candlesticks in the middle of the chancel.

These candles are put out one after the other, one at the

end of each psalm: they are like small and fragile loves which are snuffed out. Only one candle is left burning, at the top of the candlestick, when we intone the *Benedictus*. Like Christ abandoned by all His apostles. Even the altar candles are then extinguished.

Sister Gemma, who has come out of the kitchen for this service, hides the last candle behind the altar.

And we are surrounded by thick darkness, from without and from within. We've reached the heart of darkness. The black hand pressed against the heart. Death by suffocation has never been nearer, nor our complete acquiescence to darkness, despite the terrible anguish and terror, the urge to scream.

Jerusalem, Jerusalem, come back to the Lord your God.

Sister Gemma moves slowly out of sight with the last candle. Her hesitant stride, bowed back and cowed look. The flame flickering in her hand.

Neither beauty nor radiance. She has become disembodied. It is because she bears our sins. She is transpierced because of our sins. We are healed by her wounds. She bears our sickness. Our sorrows weigh heavy upon her.

The overwhelming weight of the house has been lifted from Mother Marie-Clotilde's shoulders. She feels miraculously light and calm, almost irresponsible, reassured. She congratulates herself — what a good idea it was to send Sister Gemma to her mortification in the kitchen. The strange ways of salvation.

At the conclusion of mass on Holy Saturday Sister Gemma goes to fetch the candle hidden behind the altar, according to the ritual. Sister Gemma's scream! Her panic, her whitened lips. She produces a charred, extinguished candle.

I'm certain that something awful has happened to

Joseph, thinks Sister Julie. This burnt-out candle is surely a sign of the devil.

Mother Marie-Clotilde has hastily relit the candle.

The small flame flutters once again. Hope of resurrection is restored to us. Sighs of relief. But for Sister Julie all hope has been shattered behind the altar in the night, where someone, hiding behind Sister Gemma's back, blew out the candle in her hand.

An immense silence spreads over the kneeling nuns and the entire chapel. Someone makes a racket in the choir loft to recall the earthquake that followed Jesus' death. Those who were dozing are abruptly wakened. All that remains is to retire in silence.

The altar stays bare in the chapel that has been emptied of all eucharistic presence. The unveiled cross alone is offered to our adoration.

It's winter. Fresh snow blocks the windows. That accounts for the cold bluish light that prevails here. The sun must be shining outside, snow surely crackles underfoot. No one has set foot outside the shanty for at least a week.

All the cracks between the wall boards have been stuffed with old wet newspapers kneaded like dough. We now have only to sleep, snugly rolled up in sleeping bags. No longer know if it's day or night. Stave off cold, hunger and thirst as long as possible.

Can this be a different shanty? Philomène and Adélard are squatters. They come from some unknown place, travelling through the woods with their two children on their backs in squaw fashion. The man and woman are hitched to their belongings like huskies: a large strap attached around their necks and shoulders, they pull tarpaulin-covered sleds, straining and muttering incomprehensible words in an unknown tongue. Their protruding eyes, the whites glittering, roll from right to left, from left to right. They are terrified, crafty and wicked, on the alert for the slightest noise. They keep watch on the forest, on the lookout for hidden beasts and men. It's the men they fear most. They sometimes curse them. Pursued, filled with hate, gifted with greater life than anyone else on earth, repositories of secrets, they are looking for a shanty where they can organize their feasts, their cult, their ceremonies and their still, near a village deprived of alcohol and governed by a priest. Born to live off the desires of men and women, they are capable of arousing all the hungers and thirsts imprisoned in the hearts of sleeping villages. They know how to laugh and live too strongly, and mate with a cat-like din. They choose their shanties at a distance, mark off their territory, deposit their offspring and baggage there, sometimes hastily burying both in the frozen earth (fetus and newborn embalmed in moonshine), in a hole dug under the floor of the shanty. Sometimes the man and woman, too closely pressed by the inhabitants of a village suddenly turned against them, are compelled to flee in dire haste.

Perhaps this is the first of the long succession of the shanties they have occupied? An abandoned sap-house or forgotten hunter's camp. The original shanty, with the single sleeping bag eaten away by field mice spread on the floor in the middle of the room. A big old rusty stove on bandy legs. Huge black cauldrons used for boiling maple syrup. Thin grey paddles, once so useful for spreading maple taffy on the snow. All the old but still usable material has been left there in a heap. The moonshiners are inventive and capable of everything.

If you have the courage to look inside the shanty and study every detail; if you breathe in deep gusts of the mustiness like that of warm stables and rotting seaweed that rises from the sleeping bag laid in the middle of the room, you know this is the original place.

Two peaceful giants sleep, wrapping their cold and

trembling children in their double warmth.

You might think you'd found your way back to the womb, with the father's strength guarding you. But when the father fights with the mother, he ruthlessly drives the children from their sleeping bag.

"Get out, you little bastards!"

The battle between the parents can go on all night long. Or all day. All the children can do to warm themselves is run barefoot about the fireless kitchen, clad in short, wide, stiff shirts cut from empty flour sacks and sewn with coarse stitching. A hole for the head, two for the arms. You can still read the half-faded red and blue letters on the little boy's back or the little girl's tummy:

Five Roses.

The parents are ogres. They have lit a fire in the stove and let their grub simmer. Now they hungrily devour the shiny meat smelling of burnt fat and the potatoes and lard, for days on end. They eat from blue-speckled enamel plates. They throw back their heads to drink right from the glass jugs. They wipe their mouths, chins, necks and chests with their greasy hands.

"Boiled potatoes and molasses! It's all the damn little bastards need. Salt pork is for grown-ups,"

proclaims Adélard, choking with laughter.

"Kids, kids, kids,"

clucks Philomène as if calling chicks.

She places a plate of cold potatoes floating in syrup on the floor. The children eat by the fistful the potatoes streaming with molasses. All sticky and content, they dream of returning to the warmth of the sleeping bag while the stove goes out.

The ogres, the giants lie down again, defend their downy, greasy lair, throwing firewood at the legs and toes of the little boy and girl to drive them away. They roar with laughter and embrace once more, to snore almost immediately.

The children alternate between blissful love and maddening hate for the masters of bed and stove, the lords of food and famine, supreme ministers of caresses and blows.

Huddled up against each other, the little boy and girl silently promise mutual alliance and fidelity, desiring with all their might to resist together the powers of winter and the shanty.

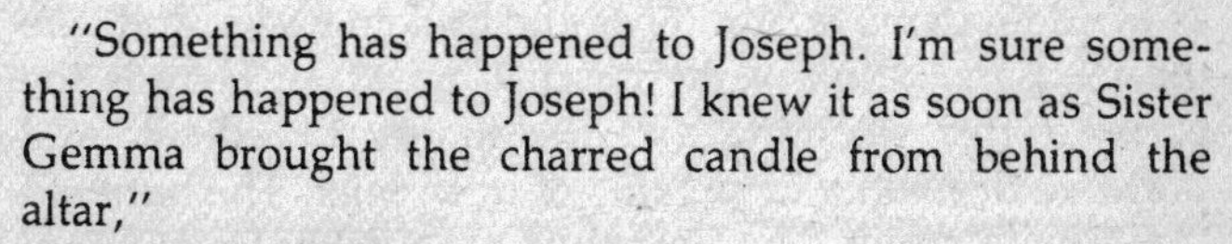

"Something has happened to Joseph. I'm sure something has happened to Joseph! I knew it as soon as Sister Gemma brought the charred candle from behind the altar,"

bewails Sister Julie.

"Sister Julie blew the candle out! I'm sure it was she! I recognized her burning breath. Look, I still have a red mark on my cheek. Here on the right. Do you see it?"

Lenten silence is shattered by complaints and accusations.

My daughters deserve to be punished. And they shall be punished. We'll have to see about Sister Gemma. As for Sister Julie, her punishment has already begun. I will in no way try to stop her believing that her brother . . . Although I have in my hands formal proof that the brother is perfectly well. May Holy Week follow its course and draw to a close in good order! No letter or missive whatsoever is to be given to the girls in my charge during the entire Lenten season, right up to Easter Sunday, after high mass. Thus our Holy Rule would have it. I am the Superior of this convent. I faithfully guard my daughters' secrets, silent as the grave. The mail that has been piling up since Ash Wednesday has been opened, processed and censored by my care, to be given to them in the proper time and place.

Amen.

May the ceremonies take place as foreseen:

The Feast of light
The Feast of water
The Blessing of the baptismal water
The Solemn Mass of the resurrection.

I arose, and am still with Thee, alleluia: Thou hast laid Thy hand upon Me, alleluia: Thy knowledge is become wonderful, alleluia, alleluia.

Alleluia, my Sisters! The word is restored to us, as well as freedom to move our knees and broken backs, and take the food and drink of the paschal breakfast. Here is the barley coffee steaming and the lumpy tweed-coloured porridge drowning in streams of fresh milk. The buttered toast smells sweet. The fast is broken. Alleluia, my Sisters! Here is the long awaited mail, set out in full view before each plate.

Therefore let us feast, not with the old leaven, nor with the leaven of malice and wickedness, but with the unleavened bread of sincerity and truth.

Alleluia, Sister Julie, open it now, the letter that's addressed to you alone, the blue airmail form postmarked: *Somewhere in England*. You are about to find out everything, girl of little faith and hope who doubted God's goodness. Your brother is well. He is on his way back to you to introduce you to his war-bride, her long legs, her turned-up nose, her cockney accent and her little brown stoneware teapot. The girl's name is Piggy. Which means "little pig".

This is a great mystery. They already form one and the same flesh. God decided it thus (Piggy being a Catholic, although English).

He that loveth his wife, loveth himself: for no man ever hated his own flesh, but nourisheth and cherisheth it; as also Christ doth the Church: for we are members of His body, of His flesh, and of His bones.

But it's beyond a nun's understanding, when all that she knows of her brother's body is his hands and face, or maybe even his bare feet in the summer, when in the limpid stream water, on the grey pebbles . . . But for the rest, a brother remains no more than male clothing to his sister, impenetrable and closed, set upon a man's form, mysterious and secret, his heart disguised, his virility hidden. And now that man, your brother, has no secrets from his wife. His entire manly body, in its most intimate details, is now offered and given over to the naked body of his young spouse, likewise known and visited by her husband, your brother Joseph. Like Christ and His Church. Alleluia, my Sister! This is a great sacrament, whatever we as nuns may guess of it in the secrecy of our bodies, filled with repugnance as we must be. The union of man and wife has been elevated to the rank of a sacrament by God Himself. God, without Whom all of that would be mere hellish fornication. Rejoice, Sister Julie! Your temptations, all lusts of the flesh appeased according to the laws of our Holy Church. Alleluia! May the Lord bless their union and cause it to bear fruit as rapidly as possible.

"Aunt Julie of the Trinity, pray for us."

Sister Julie has put her brother's letter back in the envelope. Twice she has asked for more porridge and gulped it down greedily. She has wiped her mouth on her sleeve, given a sigh of satisfaction, then a roar! She has begun to pound the table with her fists. She repeats with a voice that no longer seems to be her own:

"I'll be Goddamned! I'll be Goddamned!"

A succession of imprecations now flows forth, not only from her lips, but from every part of her body, as if she had become ventriloquous.

Wild, broken curses chop and jostle each other. But three perfectly clear words are pronounced again and again, like a leitmotiv.

"Damn! Jesus! Shit!"

Note the extraordinary position of this girl's tensed body, curved like an arc, her head almost touching her heels. It is completely beyond the powers of nature . . .

intones the old but new chaplain in a bleached voice to the Mother Superior. Both of them, the chaplain and the Superior, suddenly come alive, suddenly filled with fever and strange life after so many dull grey days.

"Be careful, Father. She's looking at you now!"

Too late: Sister Julie's gaze rests on the chaplain for an instant, perfectly flat, empty, saffron-coloured.

Unable to move or lower his eyes, the chaplain implores God in a whisper to shatter the air between Sister Julie and himself, in order to detach him from this look that casts its spell on him, crucifying him on his chair.

But before Sister Julie turns her head away, her mouth full of curses and blasphemy, the old chaplain thinks he understands what makes her gaze insufferable. The pupil of her eye is horizontally slit, like a wolf's.

They put me to sleep by force, tied me down and stuck an intravenous needle in the crook of my arm. Doctor Painchaud is to come at once. His horn-rimmed glasses crushing the tiny nose on his round pink face. He takes care not to meet my eye.

The Superior, her snout wiggling as if stealthily taking a good whiff of some poisoned, sulphurous flower, is convulsed with pleasure. Terror and guilt heighten her agitation.

The new chaplain (the former, reduced to absolute nothingness thanks to me, hanged himeslf) doesn't appear to be in very good health. Grey complexion, scowling eyes, thin, scarce hair parted in the middle like an old and drooping Sacred Heart. But surely no gleaming heart beats beneath that dirty undershirt he wears buttoned up to his chin.

They are afraid of me because my eyes are yellow, like

my mother's and my grandmother's. An entire line of viper-eyed women from over in the old country, set ashore three hundred years ago, powers and spells their only baggage, to couple with the devil from generation to generation. Or at least choosing the man the most like him, with a black or red beard, maleficent spirit and lustful body. Recognizing him, when the time came, among all the men for miles around.

They put me to sleep and cast me down into a black hole. Here I am at the bottom of a well. I have what I need to live and dream. If I half open my eyes, I see my guards observing me. They undoubtedly think they are out of danger, having put me away as a safety measure.

I have all the time I need. The deep place of dreams. The dead appear to me, make me believe in their eternal life. The hereafter is inhabited by phantoms and spectres. The soul's immortality has no other source. *A tale told by an idiot*. Reverend Fathers, reverend Sisters, don't you think it's enough to make you lose your faith? You think you've disabled me, rendered me harmless? Asleep, stretched out on this infirmary bed, thrown overboard into a night of heavy sleep. My evil geniuses watch over me. My very presence in this convent, drugged and bound as I am, remains total and malevolent.

You are all there, all three of you, spying on me, hanging on my slightest word. Twice, a contraction of my throat and chest: the cry escaping.

"She's calling her brother. Do you hear how she calls him?"

I call Joseph from the bottom of an empty well with green and rusty walls of mossy stone. Far off in the depths of the earth, the babbling of a hidden spring.

"Joseph! Joseph! It's me, Julie!"

The echo is terrible here. My voice is immediately sent back, cavernous and icy. Sound waves echoing on to infinity, Jo-o-o-seph-seph! Like a nasty drawn-out laugh slowly dying away.

I scream insults that immediately come back to me in an indescribable cacophony. Not one of the reproachful angry words I address to my brother reaches him; they fall back on me to kill me. I think of my brother as a dead man harnessed to a little English pig. Piggy, Piggy-Wiggy, my little slut, go get yourself stuffed in your pigsty by anyone you choose, but don't count on my brother to . . . Joseph, Joseph . . .

"Pray, my Sisters. Pray. She is screaming her brother's name again, like a woman possessed."

The Superior crosses herself, and the entire convent makes the sign of the cross with her.

Soon the very sound of Sister Julie of the Trinity's voice passes over to the other side of the world. Those who watch over her no longer hear or see anything.

A nun, her clothes in disorder, lies there, tied to a bed in the infirmary. She sleeps profoundly, completely withdrawn. A very old corpse that you wouldn't dare touch for fear it would disintegrate to ashes. A shell. Nothing more than a dead nun's effects lying there, parcelled with string before our eyes. The image of a nun.

The beautiful golden pine partitions. Here and there knots the colour of peach-stones. The room's timber-work clearly visible (just a wainscoting of boards) with roughly squared timbers. The ceiling, the underside of the roof, proves to be burning hot in summer, freezing cold in winter. Snow, rain, wind, grass or sand. Every degree of cold, heat, dryness or humidity, softness or roughness, is perceived by the masters of the house like the temperature of their bodies or the texture of their skins. When you have lived so intimately with the seasons, it is easy to tell what the weather will be just by blinking your eyes and scrutinizing the north, or to make hail at will by giving the water a stir.

The extraordinary headboard of the parents' bed, its shadow thrown up onto the wall. The light of the candle set on a chair near the bed. Iron lace in curlicues and royal lilies on the bed and repeated in shadow on the wall.

The mother, her crown of mustard-coloured hair just out of curlers, the violet and red patchwork quilt pulled up to her chin, her fat arms crossed behind her neck on the bare pillow. Her red mouth, with its white teeth, proclaims the strict fundamental laws of sorcery. She is talking to the father.

"Get yourself out of bed, you old devil. You broke in the girl, I must take care of the boy's ceremony. It's time."

In black letters on the wall, mingling with the garlands of the bed's shadow, the oracle delivered from the beginning of time:

THE GREATEST SORCERER AND MAGICIAN
IS HE
WHO IS BORN OF THE MOTHER AND THE SON

The old devil shrugs his shoulders and scornfully spits on the floor, feigning indifference. He says he's going to take a walk down to the village. He dons his black hat, stained with sweat in a halo all along the outer band. He goes out and slams the door.

Philomène calls Adélard back and warns him to beware of the village girls.

Adélard stops on the rise of sand and pebbles. Philomène speaks just under his nose. They accuse each other of infidelity, pummel each other. Then they burst out with joy and laughter.

They grasp each other roughly, let themselves fall to the ground, roll together to the bottom of the slope, screaming with laughter each time a pebble hurts them, ripping their dust-covered clothing.

Adélard must scour the bushes in the darkness for quite a while to find his hat. He wipes it on his dirty sleeve, sets it on the back of his head. He goes off towards the village, whistling, and limping slightly — a stone, bigger than the others, had struck him on the ankle.

Philomène bathes her wounds at the pump. She takes a

healthy gulp from the jug that had been left on the table. Enormous, puffing, her pink dress soiled by the sand, ripped and torn, blood leaking from the corner of her mouth, from her shoulder and her knees.

She summons her son in a thunderous voice.

"Joseph, Joseph," moans a broken, curiously childlike voice.

"Look, she's waking up. Listen to her moan! She's calling her brother."

They have unbound Sister Julie. On her wrists, the mark of the straps that held her down. On the back of her hands, very clear, in scarlet, two capital J's.

Mother Marie-Clotilde and the chaplain fall to their knees, murmuring the name of Jesus. Is not the holy initial clearly inscribed on each of Sister Julie's hands?

Sister Julie continues to complain in a barely audible voice, contemplates her hands with insistence and repeats tirelessly:

"Julie, Joseph, Joseph, Julie!"

The doctor makes a sudden move which barely surprises him. His index finger writing on Sister Julie's forearm. Letters appear distinctly. You can read Julie and

Jeannot. Two names interlacing each other, as if engraved with a knife on a tree trunk.

The doctor dashes out of the infirmary. You can hear his footsteps sounding in the corridor and on the stairs. Silence. Then the front door shuts heavily.

Jeannot: that is what the doctor's mother used to call him when he was a child.

The adolescent's long lean body makes its way towards the bed with its black curlicues of twisted iron. He holds his head high, seemingly contemplating a precise point beyond the clapboard wall, as though his gaze were attracted by something situated outside the shanty, even beyond the forest, somewhere very far away, beyond the reach of Philomène and Adélard.

He drinks the bitter-tasting stuff and sets the red cup down on the table. His hand begins to shake. His forehead is drenched with perspiration. He vomits a thick liquid and long filaments of green grass on the floor.

His sleepwalker's tread now guides him towards the bed set in the middle of the chalk circle. It seems to him that the approach is endless though the room is tiny. As though he were unable or unwilling to arrive at the enormous bed decked out as a catafalque. The maternal body laid out beneath the quilt, the black abyss concealed there. A strange faceless head of frizzy hair emerges on the dark blue and dirty grey striped pillow.

The litanies have been going on for quite a while. But the boy, who is still walking, makes no progress, cannot achieve the necessary state of frenzy. He finds the sound of the voices too high-pitched, recognizes among them familiar voices of certain villagers.

Candles have been set alight at the four corners of the bed. There is no air here. The flames are perfectly still. The bed seems to move away from him as the boy advances. Out of reach, he thinks. Too far off in space. The curly lemon head becomes tiny and far off, the body under the quilt more opaque and heavier, inaccessible.

His knee touches the quilt. Behind him the incantations are multiplied to infinity. No voice or sound is in unison with another. It is extremely difficult to grasp the meaning of the litanies, but the obsessive repetition of certain words exalts and comforts him. Bulls, eagles, roosters and serpents are invoked like gods, earnestly beseeched to lend him their virile strength, that the law be accomplished, that he lie with his mother.

The boy slips rather than falls onto the bed. He pulls the blanket (so slowly that his hand seems at each instant unmoving) and unveils the naked, painted body. This is where life began, this is where life must end.

The child stretches out upon the land of his birth. The mother gently disengages herself and turns her son's body over. She lies down on him, abandons herself to fondling him, with caresses more tender than any she has ever lavished on anyone. The child cries. Says he is cold and frightened.

Someone in the room screams that the sorceress has lost her powers, and that her son is a . . .

The din becomes deafening. The litanies lose all sense and rhythm.

The faithful have been carefully prepared for this moment; bewitched, drugged, according to the rules, gently led to the edge of the bed for the promised scene, the consummation between the mother and son, the trespass across the forbidden boundary: but they are now brutally wakened on the very brink of ecstasy. The earth gives way under their feet. Above all, not to be caught in the act, so close to original sin. There, on that bed decked out for lying-in-state. That woman and her son. Flee. Flee from the shanty forever.

It's every man for himself!Mingling with the villagers, the hasty departure of the offended gods, who have been disturbed for nothing. Beating of wings, crowing, mooing, hissing. All the exasperated divinities of the litanies retire in great confusion.

In the ensuing silence, Philomène's wail of fury.

The devil had remained in the shanty. He hears the woman's anger, sees the boy's chagrin. He laughs so hard he twists his ribs.

Léo-Z. Flageole, the new chaplain of the ladies of the Precious Blood, is seventy-three years old. A long career as chaplain for nuns and monks behind him. An almost infallible skill when it comes to detecting Satan at work in the soul of any penitent, male or female, kneeling before him in the confessional. They say he can trace the very shadow of sin along the most confused paths with the nose of a good hunting dog. He eats sparingly and hardly sleeps at all — it pleases him to live in a state of physical and nervois exhaustion favourable to the wonders of saintliness or hell.

A few worn, dog-eared books that have been read and reread (along with the breviary and the Holy Gospel) comprise his entire library. *The Life of Mother Catherine of Saint Augustine, Hospitaller of Mercy in New France, The Life of the Holy Priest of Ars*, Sprenger and Institor's *Malleus Maleficarum* take their places alongside the works of well-known demonologists like Bodin, Boguet and de Lancre. On the night table, his bedside book, *The Mystical Life of Mme Brault*, just published in Montreal.

The new chaplain has for years known by heart the pages of Saint Augustine and Saint Thomas of Aquinas concerning demonology.

The chaplain has spent the day in prayer and fasting (just drinking a little water): and now his long sleepless night is a blazing one. He reads and takes notes, cunningly preparing himself for any apparition or nocturnal terror.

It happened early in the morning, shortly before matins and *laudes*.

Sister Julie of the Trinity is suddenly in the chaplain's room. She jumps onto the foot of the bed and stands there staring at the chaplain. He sits propped up on a pile of pillows: all leanness, withered flesh, old brittle bones. He tries to retreat, shrinks back, chin on his knees. Sister Julie, immobile, dominates him from her full height. Her black pupil is a streak in her eye, seemingly petrified like the two hands of a watch stopped one on the other at the most fixed and unbearable point of time.

Léo-Z. Flageole hears a voice like that of Sister Julie, although Sister Julie is still standing on the bed, impassive, apparently not even breathing.

"Do you want to see what's in my family baggage, Father?"

She bends over slowly and stiffly, and pulls from under her skirts, from between her thick nun's shoes, a little antique mole-coloured suitcase, its catch rusty, its leather thin and cracked.

Two small coverless earthenware jugs fall from the suitcase and roll on the bed. The first contains a kind of thick, greasy ointment. The second a fine black powder, sand or ashes, that doesn't slide out or spill on the bed. There follow immediately armfuls of dried herbs, a linen scapulary bound by a cord, a tiny perfectly mummified toad, and two yellowed sacred hosts welded together so as to form a kind of seal.

Fear keeps the chaplain deep in his bed, prevents him from moving or crying out. The desperate desire to melt into the wood of the bed, there behind his back, to inlay himself, to shut himself up forever, to recoil until the wood absorbs him, takes him in, imprisons him, like a deposit of crumbling chalk.

"Do you wnat to see the family underwear, Father?"

She lifts up her skirt, slips her robe over her head, pulls off the wimple and cornet with a brusque gesture, defrocks herself in a trice. For an instant she appears in the slip and camisole of the Sisters of the Precious Blood, then strips completely in a flash. And a robust woman, glaring in her pink dress and yellow hair, appears in the place of Sister Julie, who has suddenly disappeared. Only the nun's clothing, piled on the floor near the bed, bears witness to her recent presence in the chaplain's room.

Nevertheless Sister Julie's voice persists, intoning the endless nomenclature of her strange genealogy.

Sister Julie of the Trinity begot by Philomène Labrosse, called la Goglue, on the one hand . . .

The woman in pink smiles, immediately bunches up her short dress, slips it over her head. The trembling chaplain has just time to glimpse two black armpits and enormous breasts. Now another woman looms up, smaller, in a long skirt and stiff collar, as if she'd been inside the womain in pink, the woman in pink being empty and hollow like a lampshade, made just to contain another, smaller woman, older in time, who in turn gives birth to another woman. A nest of women. Russian dolls nested each in the other.

"Félicité Normandin (called la Joie) begot, on the one hand, by Malvina Thiboutôt, begot on the one hand by Hortense Pruneau, begot on the one hand by Marie-Flavie Boucher, begot on the one hand by Céleste Paradis (called la Folle), begot on the one hand by Ludivine Robitaille, begot on the one hand by Marie-Zoé Laframboise, begot on the one hand by Guillemette-Anastasie Levasseur, begot on the one hand by Victoire Desjardins, begot on the one hand by Charlotte Focas, begot on the one hand by Zénobée Simoneau, begot on the one hand by Elzire Francoeur, begot on the one hand by Mathurine Soucy, begot on the one hand by Salmoé Voisine, begot on the one hand by Rosalie Jameau, begot on the one hand by Barbe Hallé, born about 1645 at La Coudray, Beauce, France, (her husband never could get on with her because she was a witch), on the one hand and on the other . . .

"I'm giddy," thinks the chaplain.

An entire line of women reproduce themselves before him, infinitely, smaller and smaller and more and more old-fashioned. The last (Barbe Hallé) is no bigger than his thumb. (Her minute bonnet, her tiny scarf.) She half-opens her chest, lets her heart fall out, fine as a raspberry seed, lets it run on the chaplain's sheets like a scarlet insect driven by a prodigious vitality and gifted with malice.

Women's clothes pile up on Léo-Z. Flageole's bedside rug. A poignant feminine odour escapes from them, rises up towards him.

Sister Julie's voice becomes impatient, repeats louder, detaching each syllable:

"And, on the other hand . . ."

No choice but to give in to the facts. He is there, in the room. With all His great height. His goat's beard. His almond eyes. His face like a knife blade. A nonchalance incomparable, in laughter and mockery. He tramples the pile of dresses on the floor with His feet to extract all their perfume, under the nose of the fainting chaplain.

He speaks in a stentorian voice:

"My creatures, all my superb creatures, my wives and daughters for three centuries . . ."

His laugh, mingled with that of Sister Julie, breaks out like a hurricane in the chaplain's room. While matins are rung at the other end of the convent.

Hodie, si vocem ejus audieritis
Nolite obdurare corda vestra
Sicut in exacerbatione secundum diem
Tentationis in deserto
Ubi tentaverunt me patres vestri
Probaverunt et viderunt opera mea

intone the sleep-befuddled nuns. Their muted steps pass before the chaplain's door. Inside the room, the devil picks up all the dresses left on the floor, piles them on his arm, takes the little mole-coloured suitcase and says he's going to bring it all to the Sisters' wardrobe.

Matins and *laudes* end; the chaplain still can't bring himself to interrupt the desperate but methodical search he's undertaken throughout the room. He is looking for a tiny raspberry seed, mislaid on his sheets by Barbe Hallé, born in 1645 in . . .

I must wax while my mother wanes.

Sister Julie of the Trinity stretches out in her nun's bed. She forgets her rage and resentment over her brother's marriage and rejoices in her strange power to haunt the entire convent.

They have confined her to a tiny room adjacent to the infirmary, a kind of white enameled pharmacy lined with shelves crowded with empty jars and vials.

Léo-Z. Flageole confers with Mother Marie-Clotilde, and then proclaims forty-eight hours of perpetual adoration. Day and night, at the sound of the bell, every hour a new guard takes the place of the old. Each sister in turn must spend an hour on her knees before the Holy Sacrament, its whiteness exposed in the golden monstrance.

Let us pray, my Sisters! Let us pray, that the convent be saved from the danger that threatens. A ravening wolf, invisible yet present in the shadows, prowls about the convent. Perhaps he has already made his way inside, moaning, ferocious, wounded by God, screaming and imploring, seeking out our souls to devour them, doomed to eternal longing.

Sister Julie has just time to return to the shanty before it is too late. On the mountain of B . . . things are about to begin happening precipitately, taking their course. Quick! While the entire convent is confined to the chapel by the perpetual adoration.

Melting snow and mud on the kitchen floor. Big, muddy tracks near the door.

Philomène is sitting in a rocking-chair that cracks and squeaks, her pink dress more faded than ever, her wide, bare feet flat on the floor, her black nails. On her head a red woolen helmet that makes her face seem like a white moon.

She jumps to her feet. The chair rocks for a while behind her, gradually slows down and becomes still.

"Nobody's ever insulted me like that!"

A public insult. Her son had failed her before the assembled faithful prepared by herbs and moonshine for the realization of their heart's deepest desire: the celebration of incest on the witch's black iron bed. Such is the law; that the darkest demon ever promised to the world be born of the son and the mother. This unique son will inherit the world. *He shall drive all nations like a herd, with his rod of iron*.

Joseph had transgressed the law. Vomited the herbs and moonshine on the shanty floor. He ran away from the shanty. He hasn't been back for several days now. Impotent. My son is impotent. Too weak to bear the vertiginous approach of love. He has gravely offended me, his mother and spouse, mistress of good and evil, supreme venomous flower of the night.

Men and women were dragged away from their daily lives, removed from their parish like frogs fished out of their native stoup, driven by night to the mountain of

B . . . trembling with fear, called by their true names, never before pronounced, revealed at last in the silence of their blood. They came here to see life burst open. Led to the highest point of expectation and desire, they were brutally released, abandoned to their own devices. They had to return to their village empty-handed, hope and faith betrayed. The ultimate magic hadn't taken place. The promise had not been kept. The sorceress and her master had deceived them, led them into temptation and left them stranded, brutally awakened with nothing left but fright and guilt.

And now, in the secret of their homes, they curse the sorceress caught in the act of failure and scandal.

Philomène says the village corrupted her son. The air people breathe down there is vitiated. Joseph had already been led astray, long before the ceremony, by the people of the valley.

Philomène has let none of her son's comings and goings escape her notice. Apparently as impassive as stone, she is engaged in seeing. From the top of the mountain, every far-off image is enlarged and magnified up to thirty times beneath her gaze. Like a bird of prey, she can discern a fieldmouse moving in the grass behind the beadle's house.

The eye of the sorceress probes the shadow in which the boy is hiding. Her maternal gaze follows him as he pursues his quest among men. Sometimes, at night, he thinks he feels his mother gliding over him, grazing the village roofs, adopting the silent flight of owls. Joseph knows that she can swoop down on him at any moment and devour him with a few blows of her beak, to throw up afterwards the child's bones, nails, hair and teeth in a pile.

Full daylight brings some reassurance to Joseph, but the moves he makes to spy on village and country dwellers are cramped and awkward. He examines and sniffs them from a distance, hidden in a ditch, behind a shed, in the bushes along the road, in the shelter of a snowbank in winter. Sensitive, easily swayed, he is filled with delight, his eyes, ears and nose rejoice in every gesture, form, colour, sound and odour given off by the monotonous and pious life of the people of the valley. They are, every one of them, victims of the poverty of the land, the whims of the four seasons, and of the laws of the Church and its priest.

At night, when mist rises from the river and covers the village, Philomène has only to listen carefully through patches of downy fog (like someone listening under water): she perceives, in the secrecy of wooden houses and the creaking of bedsprings, the calm or restless breathing of the sleepers she haunts. In the freedom of their dreams, they adore and curse her in turn.

Philomène is alone in the dark, lying on her back.

On the other side of the partition, the daughter's cries and the father's laughter. Those things they do together, both of them, lying in the pallet. What the father obtains by force alone. What the daughter learns to fight off, then to desire, to crave, at the very gates of death. The enchantment of violence. The girl struggles, claws, bites and screams, until hell shakes her through with happiness, leaves her inert on the straw like a corpse.

Satan claims horror alone leads to truly great voluptuousness, and that a good sorceress must have known voluptuousness and hatred. There will soon be two witches in the house: too many. The elder must disappear.

The most important things said between the father and daughter are expressed wordlessly. In absolute silence, in the blackest of nights. The language of body to body, its eloquent adequacy.

Dear Satan, my father and spouse. (His great manly waters in me, his laugh like big bells chiming.) Teach me everything! Perversity. Afterwards I will leave you without regret. As far as hatred is concerned, you can count on me. I must go debauch my brother Joseph, who has fled to the woods because he fears my mother, the witch.

"I'm leaving, Julie. I won't stay here with that woman in the house."

I, Julie, daughter of . . . I'll succeed where my mother failed. Change a child into a man. My love for Joseph is that great. I will be his woman. I will avenge him, and myself with him. Take vengeance against Philomène and against you too, my dear master. Go away with Joseph, set ourselves up on our own to rule over a large territory, making moonshine and magic. Being young together, letting the dead bury the dead, far behind us.

I'm half a head taller now than she. I can see very clearly the black roots mingling with strings of white in her yellowish hair, hanging like wispy moss down to her shoulders. I will take all her secrets from her: such is the law. The moonshine recipe, herbs and unguents, the art of predicting the weather and of stirring water to make hail, the power of making the wind turn, the possibility of turning anger into thunder and lightning. And boldness enough to set free a whole cohort of hallucinated dancers under a full moon at the bottom of a ravine, defying all together the edicts of the diocese, as one must to pass over to the other side of the world.

The impure alcohol wreacks havoc all over the county. Several people are dead. Two men are blind. A warrant has been issued. The police have received an order to search for hidden stills, to destroy them and arrest the distillers. The inhabitants' tongues are loosened. They speak in low voices of the abominations that are committed on the mountain of B . . . They even go so far as to evoke the magic herbs which, taken with alcohol, can bring on visions.

It is the silence that strikes you when you enter the shanty. The man and woman haven't lit the lamp. They drink in small gulps, slowly. There is a glass jug between them, on the table. You can read on the green label: *One of the Heinz 57 varieties*. Three other jugs are lined up under the table, within arm's reach. The shutters are closed. The man and woman swore to empty the remaining jugs themselves, rather than lose them by leaving the shanty.

They have already nailed the old rickety shutters tight with diagonal boards.

It's been several days since the still was working in the cellar. It has been deeply buried and covered over with beaten earth. The herbs have been pulled from their pots and incorporated into the booze.

"This mixture is a great success," declares Philomène.

For a fleeting instant, the woman swigging down her drink is touched by a desire to flee. Too late. The moment has already passed. The desire to flee has already gone. Some exaggerated slowness in Philomène's muscles and nerves, in her very desire to flee, prevented her from getting up and running out of the shanty at once when an inner urge gave the order to do so.

Adélard, sitting opposite, motions her to empty the jug. The man changes before her eyes. His face becomes ever more closed and opaque.

The woman drinks. She places just a little space of drunkenness, like the alveolus of air in a bird's egg, between herself and the lurking danger. All around this refuge where visions come so easily, the thin, rough wooden walls of the shanty, like a shell.

Nausea.

Delirium.

No lamp is lit in the room and yet the woman sitting near the table, her elbows resting on the oilcloth, is blinded by light. Vainly she places her hands over her eyes, covers her face with her woolen sweater; the light (her center and core) is situated in her head and illuminates the entire countryside.

Men, women, children and animals file past in a torrent of flashes. The entire forest, the village and the countryside slip between her fingers like trout. They accuse Philomène as they pass. They point their fingers at her.

"There she is! That's la Goglue!"

If they are questioned, they will tell all to the police. But God alone, they think, can deliver them from their sins, by the priest's mediation. Soon they will go to confession, all of them. So great is their fear of God's wrath. Already men are dead, their entrails burned out by whisky blanc. These are the survivors: they are thrown into panic and implore God's mercy with trembling gestures.

You cannot catch them.

Here are Joseph and Julie, or rather their image. They sit side by side at the foot of a fir tree in the forest. No use trying to detain them: they fly by at the speed of light, while remaining perfectly still at the foot of their tree.

No use trying to save Malvina Beaumont either. She has taken refuge in the barn of her husband, Jean-Baptiste Beaumont, farmer. She has already lost much blood in the cured hay on which she has been lying since her return from the mountain if B . . . late yesterday evening.

Philomène can always close her eyes. But red flashes persist beneath her eyelids, as though she had been staring too long at the sun.

Outside, an unmistakeably earthly, ironshod tread mounts the sandy rise, suddenly sets all the shanty spectres to flight.

You can see the man's hat pulled down over his eyes through the cracks between the boards. He is alone. He knocks on the door. A kind of scratching rather, the usual signal. A long wait follows. You can hear the man's breath through the thin door. Once again the same scratching, the same breathing. The man goes around the shanty. Pine needles crunch beneath his step. He raps on the first kitchen shutter. Mutters the password.

"La Goglue, you there?"

He goes off towards the woods. You can hear him swearing. He disappears, comes back, begins the same stratagem without hurrying or raising his voice or even scratching harder. He goes around to the three kitchen shutters, scratching on them one after the other with his stubby nails, repeating between his teeth:

"La Goglue, you there?"

Once again the crunching of pine needles under his tread as he goes off towards the woods. A scant quarter of an hour goes by. He comes back to strike the clapboard siding with all his might, his big wide callused hands pounding out his invincible stubbornness, his pent-up despair. Unwilling, unable to resign himself to going without moonshine on that particular evening, he tirelessly repeats in a whining tone:

"La Goglue, la Goglue, you there? You there?"

Philomène is still on her chair by the table. The man's hands, breath and lamentations seem to pass through the thin panelling to touch, brush, pull and grasp her. She is ill-protected by the door's rudimentary catch and the shutter's hastily nailed brackets, desperately called upon by a man in need. For the first time Philomène learns to play dead and refuses to fulfil a desire. The most elemental caution commands her.

Two full hours pass before the man makes up his mind to return to the village.

Adélard, his entire being lifeless. His lacklustre eye, dull like pewter. He leans over Philomène and coldly contemplates her. He orders her to drink a bit more. He orders her to sleep. He stands aloof now, using "vous" when he speaks to her.

"Sleep. I want you to."

Her head falls on the table between her two outstretched arms. She sleeps at once.

Adélard picks her up, holds her standing before him for an instant. A flabby puppet. He removes her dress as one undresses a sleeping child. Her arms flap down again, her breasts wobble. Her head bobs from one shoulder to the other. Her chin falls to her chest.

He lays her out on the iron bed. Carefully paints the body in the ritual colours. The punishment has already begun in the woman's withering flesh. Having failed with her son, the mother must be sacrificed. The greatest magic did not take place. The sorceress is condemned.

Adélard hangs her pink dress on a nail on the wall. Beside the blue straw hat of her visits to Georgiana's place.

Philomène receives Adélard one last time. He fills her with cold semen. So that she may know forever that he is the cold god.

He covers the inert body with the red and violet quilt and leaves the room. He goes into the kitchen, picking up his old hat on the way. Opens the door onto the night that is drawing to a close. He fills his lungs with the wondrous air of this world, then shuts the door behind him.

He goes off along the still cool July road, his hat set back on his head, his hands in his pockets. He hums a derisive little tune. He is finished with that woman lying in the shanty, and now teases her joyously. Insinuates himself into her very sleep, summons and defies her, haunts her forever. He goes off at an easy gait.

"La Goglue, you there?"

Philomène who can no longer answer any call, Philomène from whom the departure of love can drain no tear, enjoys the prodigious acuity of her hearing, of her ears, fine and pointed.

I'm making the most of what I've got left, thinks Philomène. She delights in Adélard's diminishing tread until he has quite disappeared from the face of the earth, at the first turn of the road, through the thick undergrowth. Swallowed up by thorns and stagnant smells.

The sound of the parish church bell now rolls out over the entire countryside in long, slow, mournful strokes. Malvina Beaumont's knell tolls interminably, escapes towards the mountain of B . . ., soon reaches the shanty.

"La Goglue, you there?"

It is death calling.

The cut hay lies neglected in the fields. The country dwellers are going down to the village for Malvina Beaumont's burial. Children walk barefoot in the summer dust. Crickets' shrilling and the cicada's strident song accompany them on either side of the road.

Si iniquitates observaveris Domine:
Domine, quis sustinebit?

Malvina Beaumont's husband angrily repeats that his seventeenth child has been cast into Limbo and his wife thrown into Hell, and he just isn't going to let it go at that.

A porta inferi erue, Domine,
Animam meam.

Each one is going back over things in his heart, during the entire burial mass.

She's the one. La Goglue is responsible for everything. She's the one who brought death to Jean-Baptiste Beaumont's wife in a state of mortal sin, and to the two Lefebvre brothers, who weren't exactly in a state of grace either. A poisoner. An angel-maker. La Goglue is a sorceress. She works wonders and atrocities. She seduced us and would now push us into hell. We must be rid of her and reconcile ourselves with God before it's too late. That creature must leave the countryside as soon as possible, and her devil of a husband with her!

Dies irae, dies illa
Solvet saeclum in favilla
Teste David cum Sibylla.

The ban is categorical. No drinking place is to be opened in any village whatsoever. The temperance society, directed by the priest, made us swear never to drink. Just as women swear obedience and submission to their husbands. While the children solemnly pledge, as soon as they are ten years old, to renounce Satan, his pomp and his works.

Quantus tremor est futurus,
Quando judex est venturus,
Cuncta stricte discussurus.

We are bound by promises and bans. We are subjected to the climate's hardships and the poverty of the soil. We are held in check by the fear of sin and hell.

The world is in order: potatoes and hay give a good crop every two years, children grow tough and hardy. Ten, fifteen children to baptize in a woman's lifetime, what could be more normal? In winter, salt pork is for the men. Women and children make do with potatoes and molasses.

Rex tremendae majestatis
Quem patronum rogaturus
Cum vix justus sit securus?

Our mistake was wanting to escape our fate. We went up to the mountain of B . . . in search of a miracle. And look where it's led us now; several corpses on our hands and mortal sins welling in our conscience.

Liber scriptus proferetur
In quo totum continetur.

Back home, Jean-Baptiste Beaumont fills a jug (one of those from the shanty) with coal oil. He places a long wick in it. He packs the jug thus prepared in a kind of grey cloth haversack. The bag on his back, walking carefully, he goes off towards the mountain of B . . .

Dies irae, dies illa.

La Goglue, you there?

The church bells ring out in sonorous volleys.

Julie puts her hands over her ears. She flees into the forest, knowing with her certain knowledge what is going to happen in the shuttered shanty.

The youth's tracks are easy to follow. She runs until she is out of breath, in the ferns that burn beneath her feet. Her singed, zig-zag trail bears witness to the power to harm grass and summer greens given in heritage to Julie Labrosse, daughter of . . .

Speckled copperheads uncoil and hiss at her approach, follow her among the mossy stones and moist grass for a moment like a cortege.

The shade is cool in the heart of the forest. It is like entering water. Brambles, roots grazing the surface, dry, pointed stumps. Inextricable undergrowth everywhere. Occasional patches of moss where the black-streaked white birches grow.

Julie's forced breathing, her feet, legs, arms and face covered with scratches, her tiny plaintive cry:

"Joseph! Joseph!"

The nursing sister sent for them early in the morning. Now the three of them are together at her bedside. The Mother Superior, the chaplain and the doctor. They contemplate the signs of a strange Passion engraved on Sister Julie's lacerated face and forehead. The same capital J, once again inscribed on the back and palms of her hands. The doctor abruptly pulls back the blanket, revealing Sister Julie's clawed and scratched legs and feet.

"J for Jesus,"

murmurs the nursing sister, her gaze riveted on Sister Julie's hands. The nursing sister crosses herself with a quick tap of the thumb on her clothes-padded breast.

In a clear voice Sister Julie declares that she would gladly take a bowl of porridge, but that she urgently desires to go to the bathroom first.

Mother Marie-Clotilde stands watch in the corridor to ensure that no other nun crosses the path of this Sister

Julie, nightcap down over her ears, cowlicks sticking up in all directions, her shirt ripped and torn, her body marked by scratches and stigmata, as though she'd just escaped with her life from some wildcat battle.

The nursing sister firmly holds Sister Julie's arm as she goes off towards the washroom with a resolute gait.

The entire convent seems deserted at that hour. The large parlour, however, is noisy as a muffled hive. Fear and astonishment. Subdued, confused exclamations.

The beautiful green ferns, pride of the convent, planted in blue earthenware flower-boxes opposite the little straw chairs lined up along the parlour grille, have been mysteriously damaged during the night. The scorched broken stems seem to have narrowly escaped a fire.

Léo-Z. Flageole, carefully prepared by his great age, his meditations, his medieval dreams, and by fasting and insomnia, surrenders with terror and delight to the malfunction of all his senses and his very reason.

He observes Sister Julie, takes notes, feverishly consults his favourite demonologists, but refrains from pronouncing a final judgement on Sister Julie's case. He patiently awaits the accumulation of signs and proof, and prepares a detailed file. He dreams wide awake, night and day.

For a whole long night the chaplain persists in expecting Sister Julie in the chapel. After several hours of waiting he finally spies her, from behind, solid and mocking in the shadows, too strong-backed, too square, it seems to him, of a race too strong, too energetic. He vainly attempts to catch up with her in the right side-aisle, near Saint Michael's altar. He distinctly hears insolent laughter, suddenly stifled. There follows the sound of light steps echoing on the stairs to the rood-loft. The chaplain painfully tilts his hoary head towards the high beams from which the convent bell hangs. He perceives a strange commotion, a wild agitation, pressing and rumpling of skirts. Like a rustling and smoothing of heavy wings. The chaplain can't help thinking that Sister Julie is about to sly off from the belfry. He soon distinctly sees a nun's foot, its large black laced shoe and ribbed white woolen stockings swinging down in the air, only to disappear for good.

Léo-Z. Flageole finds himself shivering and snoring, half collapsed on his prie-dieu in the chapel choir, at about three o'clock in the morning.

The little sanctuary lamp and all the candles have been extinguished. A mortal cold reigns there; the chaplain will never completely recover from it.

Even if Léo-Z. Flageole, Mother Marie-Clotilde and the doctor remain silent, the most extraordinary news spreads through the entire convent. The nursing sister is undoubtedly partly responsible. The word "miracle" glides under every door, trickles down the walls, slips between rosary beads. Cornets have antennas, and wimples have radar. Recess brings whispers. A sniffing and scenting of the supernatural that floats in the air.

The sisters make wishes as they pass by Sister Julie's door.

They prefer to come at night, without breaking the convent silence, without even stopping. Barely slowing their pace in the corridor. Just long enough to concentrate. In whispers they implore God, or the devil. What's the difference? As long as their wish is heard and granted. The insatiable greed of those who have renounced everything in hope of the eternal miracle.

"If I just breathe the same air as she, the air seeping through the keyhole, I'll be revenged on Sister Marie-Rose who always steals my place at confession before the entire community. May the thief be confounded and severely punished."

"If my skirt just brushes the door panel shutting her in, I'll no longer always be served last in the refectory, when all that remains is the blue whey in the bottom of the pitcher, when the soup plate contains only dishwater mixed with dirt from half-washed vegetables."

"I beg you, let me die with Sister Angèle of Merici; her

red cheeks, her burning hands, her crucified beauty, all the mortal light that shines forth from her and consumes her. To be consumed with her, burn in love with her and die. Let us both die together — Sister Angèle who is condemned, and myself, who am healthy and joyous. I want to die of love! That is why I entered the convent. Extend us, both of us, on the same cross. One and the same last breath for both, in the flames of consumption and fever. Say but a word and we will die together . . . ."

The silence of the convent mumbles like the nocturnal silence of the forest. Sister Julie listens and grants their desires.

Sister Marie-Rose will come down with a bad case of diarrhoea just as she is about to enter the confessional, and Sister Antoinette will recover her rightful place at her confessor's feet. Mother Marie-Clotilde will decide to change the usual order in the refectory, and Sister Blanche will drink the creamy top of the milk every day from now on, until she is sick of it. As for Sister Marie of Bon-Secours, she will merely have to swallow some bloody spittle from Sister Angèle of Merici. She will come down with galloping consumption. And the two little sisters will expire on the same day at the same time, like one single candle blown out in a breath.

Sometimes a hollow voice whispers in Sister Julie's ear while she sleeps on a high, narrow bed like an ironing board, tucked under grey blankets in a tiny, double-locked room.

"You are my daughter and my continuation. You must possess and bewitch all these bloody swooning nuns, every last one of them."

Upon wakening, Sister Julie's joy is equalled only by her appetite.

"I want peas and salt pork! Beans and pork! Cabbage and pork! Molasses and catsup! And peanut butter too!"

The nursing sister notes all of Sister Julie's words in a little black notebook according to her orders, so that she can report to Mother Marie-Clotilde. She is astonished to discover nothing supernatural, whether edifying or maleficent.

Sister Julie's diet has been suggested by the Superior and prescribed by the doctor: milk dishes, very white, without salt or sugar.

The nursing sister, (though she was chosen for her placidity and lack of imagination) piously conserves the linen used to bathe Sister Julie's ever renewed lacerations.

"Are you collecting relics, Sister?"

Caught in the act by Sister Julie, the nurse blushes. But how can she suspect that only a desperate flight through the forest of the mountain of B . . . could so deeply claw someone's entire body.

It's no use running now. It's too dark. Impossible to find her way. Julie, out of breath and wet with sweat, leans against a tree. To wait for daylight. Tears flow, followed by violent sobs. She swallows her tears rapidly and blows her nose into leaves. Black night everywhere. Sky and earth indistinguishable. The ferocious, invisible life of the forest teeming all about her. Branches cracking, shrill voices in the grass, the nearby cry of an owl, the flight of a fieldmouse. The devourer and the devoured. Claws, teeth, piercing eyes. Male, female, love and the hunt, each creature hunter and prey in turn.

All things that fly, walk and crawl surround Julie and brush against her. In the distance, a brook lapping. A patch of phosphorescence gleams on an old tree like dozens of little lighted eyes. Suddenly two eyes loom up in the shadow, just beside Julie. Rapid breathing against her face. A vague form is there, living and breathing, two steps away from her. She screams. But before another scream answers hers, she has recognized, in the dark, the warmth of the young body, the smell of the old clothes, the rude perfume of a never-washed boy and his musky hair.

"Joseph!"

"Julie!"

They embrace like drowning victims, remain enlaced at the foot of a tree, their heads slightly turned towards the shanty, awaiting the inevitable.

Can it be that Julie really sees through the black night? For an instant, the darkness is torn apart. Or perhaps she imagines it? In a flash she makes out a dark, hairy arm. It pitches a glass jug against the shanty. Inside the jug an agitated liquid, a burning wick. On the bulge, a green label, recognizable among all others.

Night again. The inextricable forest.

A reddening gleam soon rises above the treetops, followed by a wreath of smoke in opaque rolls.

"The forest is burning,"

says Joseph.

"It's the shanty blazing like a match box,"

Julie corrects him.

Aroused from deep sleep by Jean-Baptiste Beaumont's screams of "Fire!", the villagers thought the entire mountain was going up in flames. During the night they made a chain with their ridiculous little pails of water drawn from the brook. They had to prevent the forest from burning. It was already too late for the shanty, soon nothing but smoking ashes.

They all go home in the early morning. The fire has been put out and the wind has died down. Light and purified after the sacrifice of the shanty, the village folk avoid enquiring too closely about the shanty's occupants. They are undoubtedly on the run, already in the deepest heart of the forest they never should have left.

Now the villagers have only to shut themselves up in

their houses and give thanks to the Lord for their rediscovered peace. To kneel down on the knotty kitchen floor with the family and recite the rosary, in the shadow of the cross nailed up on the wall between the enlarged portraits of relatives, sinister and mortuary.

It is only after nightfall that Joseph and Julie dare approach the smoking ruins. A bitter odour grips their throats.

"There! Dead wood! There!"

screams Sister Julie of the Trinity, while the nursing sister struggles to hold her down on the narrow bunk.

Sister Julie tosses about, extends her arm, points to something hidden in shadow at the foot of her bed. She repeats in a hollow changing voice:

"Dead wood! There!"

The charred quilt falls to dust as soon as you touch it. The parents' room no longer has a roof or walls or a floor. The twisted iron bed rises up in the open air, in the midst of tangled, charred boards. Greasy soot flies around and powders everything, clings to our feet and hands, stings our noses, burns our eyes and makes us cough. All around, the forest is a fence of burnt tree stumps and scorched, shrivelled leaves. On the ground, razed grass and pine needles in long sooty trails.

The bizarre little head, the bizarre little body, shrunken

and carbonized. A black wooden doll lies half buried in the slit mattress, sunk into the collapsed bedspring.

Flee!

Once again Joseph and Julie are running in the forest. Julie has stopped to fill her pockets with black ashes.

The nursing sister is trembling with fright. She begs to be relieved of her duties at Sister Julie's bedside. Last night, in a corner of the shadow-filled room, when only the small blue night-light was lit, Sister Julie rose up in her sleep. She extended her arm towards . . .

"And I couldn't help seeing what Sister Julie was showing me, there, at the foot of the bed."

"And what did you see, Sister?"

Mother Marie-Clotilde's voice is slightly hoarse. Her glasses are fogged, their lenses veiling her equine eyes.

"I saw a wooden idol lying on the floor, half charcoal . . ."

Mother Marie-Clotilde's voice becomes imperceptible, her gaze completely drowned.

"What makes you believe it was an idol, Sister?"

"It looked like a pagan statue carved by Negroes in Africa, like the ones you see in the missionary magazines, black as coal."

The chaplain in turn questions the nursing sister. He avoids looking at her, seemingly busy extracting from his cassock the thermal cotton that covers his chest. Handfuls of soiled cotton soon bestrew the floor all around Léo-Z. Flageole's armchair. When the nursing sister has finished her account, he motions to her to pick it all up and prepare him some fresh cotton.

The nursing sister is relieved of her vigil at Sister Julie's side. A three-day retreat, completely incommunicado, is prescribed for her. The *in pace*. Total silence. A long tête à tête with herself. To scrutinize the darkness of her soul. Meticulous distinction between dream and reality, to prepare her for a general confession of all her nightmares.

Mother Marie-Clotilde cannot help praising Léo-Z.

Flageole's wisdom.

Is it not, above all, a case of bringing the convent back to solid ground and preventing it from straying, all sails flying, on the troubled waters of the imagination?

Father Flageole fears any premature revelation of the events troubling the ladies of the Precious Blood. He must not risk being treated once again as an obsessed neurotic by doctors and superiors. Is it not better to let Sister Julie attain the extreme limit of her possession before notifying the highest religious authorities? Keep the secret, maintain his solitary state of siege against Satan (with the fragile help of Mother Marie-Clotilde and Doctor Painchaud).

Let Sister Julie be caught in the act of diabolical inebreity, before the eyes of all, and my existence will be justified at last. I'll finally be able to practise openly my true ministry, the one I have dreamed of since entering the seminary. To carry out an exorcism with full pomp, according to the ritual of the Province of Quebec. Perhaps I might also attempt the test by needles on Sister Julie's body? Patiently, conscientiously search her entire naked flesh for the *stigma diaboli*?

That night, Father Flageole had a serious asthma attack that kept him awake until the early hours of the morning. Suffocation. His heart, sprung from between his ribs, was pierced with beaming arrows and long golden needles. Thus had the Sacred Heart appeared to Saint Marguerite-Marie-Alacoque, nun of the Order of the Visitation, born in Lauthecour in 1647.

Such a divine resemblance rejoiced Father Flageole. But he nonetheless feared choking and death.

At that moment Sister Julie came to sit on the foot of the chaplain's bed. One by one she plucked the arrows and needles from his heart and covered his chest with a bandage so soft and cool that Léo-Z. Flageole felt himself immediately cured of his wounds and asthma, wrapped in sweetness. Exhausted and grateful, he was about to sink into delicious sleep when he noticed that the bandage she had slipped inside his shirt, against his chest, was none other that Sister Julie's two extended sweet and unctuous hands.

Father Flageole uttered such a cry that the entire convent woke that morning with a start, long before matins.

As for Doctor Painchaud, he really doesn't look well. He is often reduced to spending the night in a chair. Sometimes he even takes Benzedrine tablets. Anything, rather than allow himself to fall asleep. Fear devours him, fear of being suddenly aroused in the middle of the night by a terrible spectre that will crush his chest before abandoning him in the midst of amorous ecstasy.

Jean Painchaud's fatigue is so great that several of his patients can't help noticing it. His face also changes, visibly. His round pink cheeks (until now only a few little stray hairs managed to sprout there) are blackened by a heavy beard by six o'clock in the evening. He must shave twice a day. His features (soft and babyish in spite of his forty years of age) develop furrows and harden gradually.

He finally neglects all religious practices as well as the ample motherly skirts of the nuns. Yet he had sought refuge among them often over the years, having failed to find among the city women skirts deep and calm enough to hide in. The gentle odour of sour milk and faded incense! All the virgin mothers protected him (gentle battalion of saints) from the city creatures that occasionally threw him such lustful or mocking glances. Besides, at the convent he received a welcome equal to that offered to the chaplain himself, with the same reserved, respectful excitement.

Unnerved by Sister Julie's nocturnal visits, encouraged by the exuberance of his beard and the virility of his new face, Doctor Painchaud decides to ask one of his colleagues for a good address.

In a house on Saint Paul Street, two girls take care of him in turn. The first is very young and sweet, the second wise, brusque and maternal. But neither succeeds in arousing Doctor Painchaud's slumbering nature.

As he goes, the second woman encourages him to come back.

"Don't worry about tonight. It's the beer, honey. It's not your fault."

Blessed art thou among all women . . .

repeats the doctor next morning while driving his car through the maze of narrow Quebec City streets towards the convent of the ladies of the Precious Blood, his thoughts all with Sister Julie.

Full of grace, the Devil is with thee . . .

Jean Painchaud laughs at the wheel of his car. He wonders if Sister Julie really is beautiful? More than anything else in the world, he wants to know that for certain. At the same time, he is afraid to look her in the face. More than beauty, vitality and energy reign there. An extraordinary body. An unnatural face. You must face the facts: all this radiance of Sister Julie's dazzling flesh surpasses the forces of nature.

Suddenly healed, sleek and white with no traces of scratches or wounds, she sits enthroned in her bathrobe, without a bonnet, in a chair beside her sickbed, its sheets carefully folded shut like an envelope. Her tonsured hair (beginning to grow back) falls silky and mossy on her forehead and neck. When she turns her head you can admire her fine eagle's beak. Her strong white teeth protrude in a blinding smile.

"I've had enough. I want to get out of this damned house, at once. The time of my conversion is past. My brother is married. Let his piggy English girl protect him from war if she can!"

She laughs, her milky breast thrown upward. Two buttons have been torn from the collar of her bathrobe.

There can be no doubting Sister Julie's beauty now. It brings Doctor Painchaud to a kind of despair. He doesn't dare meet Sister Julie's gaze, afraid of discovering the strange pupils of which Léo-Z. Flageole has already told him.

News of Sister Julie of the Trinity's recovery spreads through the entire convent. Hope rises again. Among the kneeling, in the chapel; the sitting, in the linen-room; but above all in the infirmary, among the aging bedridden nuns covered with bedsores. At night, prayers and supplications rise up stronger than ever towards Sister Julie, still imprisoned in a tiny white room full of cold reflections, like a bathtub.

Sister Gemma alone resists, and claims the very air you touch in the convent is poisoned. If you stop there, you inhale a stagnant odour of wild iris, like the smell steaming from the swamps in springtime.

In the kitchen, food spoils as soon as it is delivered, under Sister Gemma's eyes and nose. The enormous community refrigerators break down each night, give off a smell of ammonia each morning as soon as they are opened. Vegetables rot in their burlap bags. Fruit grows over-ripe as soon as it is touched. Milk turns sour. Butter rancid. Best not to talk about the beef, almost always flabby, of a yellowish-grey hue.

Nausea, vomiting, fainting spells; Sister Gemma is ill. Soon she can swallow nothing, although the Superior forces her to eat and obstinately refuses to relieve her of her duties.

Sister Gemma is needed in the kitchen. Salvation will undoubtedly come to us through her very disgust and horror.

Sister Gemma claims the odour infecting the entire convent (no one but herself seems aware of it) emanates from the room in which Sister Julie is kept. When Sister Gemma passes by in the corridor, she smells the devil beneath the pharmacy door. She is afraid of fainting.

The chaplain of the Sisters of the Precious Blood comforts Sister Gemma. He even suggests that, by the incommensurable mystery of God's grace, it could well be that the salvation of the community rests on Sister Gemma's frail shoulders. Since she alone can detect the devil's pestilence in Sister Julie's soul, it is undoubtedly up to her to take charge of that soul, in order to redeem it from eternal death, in union with Jesus Christ our Lord.

The economy of salvation. The mystical body of Christ. Sister Gemma suffers a thousand daily deaths. Her disgust is extreme, as if she had been cast into a manure pile, to live and die there.

May I quickly become a saint and may all this be brought to end! I want to die in an apotheosis of thornless white roses, in their sweet aroma. Quickly! Very quickly, O God! I can stand it no longer. I'm at the end of my tears and fright. My God! My God, why hast Thou forsaken me? Such a long dark night. Must I die despairing? Is that what is demanded of me? O sweet God of my childhood, my Father, what has become of Thee? And the whiteness of my soul, the day I entered the convent, now it is like a crumbled holy wafer set on a dirty cloth.

Sister Julie exults. A few sudden recoveries from ulcers

and eczema, a few mysterious resorptions of cysts bring her less pleasure than the image of Sister Gemma streaming with tears, as she is able to summon her, day or night, whenever Sister Julie feels the malicious urge to do so.

The Sister Bursar (a business genius, but oblivious to all else) does her best to take care of Sister Julie and watch over her, replacing the demoted nurse.

The Sister Bursar repeats half aloud that two and two are four, like a child whistling in the dark to convince himself he's not afraid. But after several long hours of watching over Sister Julie, she begins to talk nonsense.

"I'm a realistic person, Mother. You can trust my common sense. I know chalk from Jesus. Economy, economy, Mother! Therein lies the secret of great fortunes and well-established convents. There is no such thing as a small profit. You must lay on an egg. I'm telling you! Sister Julie is as gay as a fish. I can't see what she sees, neither what nor whom, when she stares out the window — I stay behind her to watch. But I feel the effrontery getting through, on one side and on the other, from the street to the convent and from the convent to the street, through the windowpane, like a draught rising and descending . . . One rotten egg in the barrel, as anyone knows . . ."

Sister Julie has asked the Sister Bursar for pins. She has tacked her brother's wedding picture to the wall. She has stuck a number of pins into the lower abdomen of the smiling, long-limbed bride. Then, her hands hidden in the folds of her skirt, she has made several knots in her rope belt.

Patient and rested, Sister Julie then orders the Sister Bursar (who has no choice but to obey) to go fetch her some cigarettes. A package of Player's (fallen from one of the doctor's pockets) seems to be waiting on the floor, in the corridor leading to the main entry.

The Sister Bursar follows Sister Julie's instructions to a T: in no time at all she knows how to smoke. From that moment on, her life has changed.

Clouds of smoke soon billow up in the Sister Bursar's polished office. Spirals, twirls, perfect rings float up towards the ceiling. The Sister Bursar crosses her brittle legs in their ribbed stockings, very high. She repeats with delight that she now smells of tobacco like a man. Her skirts, her cornet, her underskirts, her Zouave's bloomers, her entire skin from head to toe, bear witness to the conquering virile perfume of a tobacco shop.

In a blue fog that makes her cough, the Sister Bursar treats the convent's affairs with a dexterity and assurance never before attained. Without consulting the Superior or the assistant, she grabs the telephone, a cigarette dangling from the corner of her mouth, her eyes pleated by the smoke. In the voice of a Russian basso, she wheels and deals. The community's regular, aging notary, and its broker, defeated, dumbfounded, can only follow the peremptory and strange instructions of the Sister Bursar. They sell shares, bonds and properties at at a loss, to buy at exorbitant prices moose pasture in deserted regions, and mortgage-laden buildings. They commit blunder after blunder, organizing the convent's ruin. While the Sister

Bursar goes through the shares that remain in her possession, burning all the coupons made out to "bearer".

Fury. Despair. The losses seem irreparable. The Sister Bursar is immediately demoted from her functions and shut up in the attic, amidst spider webs and novices' trunks, under green and white ropes of wreathed garlic hanging from the ceiling. Far, very far from Sister Julie's deleterious influence.

Mother Marie-Clotilde's hand trembles with anger. She double-locks the door. The Sister Bursar screams from behind the door that she is a businessman. She demands some Old Chum tobacco, a meerschaum pipe and a copper spittoon. Her stentorian voice resounds through the entire convent, bounding from one level to the other, all the way down to the ground floor.

"Only one thing counts, my Sisters. O girls of little memory, have you forgotten? I, Rose of Lima, bursar, I'm giving you back divine poverty, fallen to disuse in this convent. You must die in extreme poverty, on straw, my Sisters. Like the Christ-child in the manger. The kingdom of heaven is for the cat who can pass through the needle's eye."

Woe unto us, for Satan has descended upon us with great fury.

Mother Marie-Clotilde thinks they should inform the archdiocese immediately in order that the Grand Exorcist may come and drive the demon from the convent as quickly as possible. But Father Flageole is definitely against it; he prefers to proceed with the exorcism ceremonies himself.

All the evil comes from Sister Julie, without a doubt. What do we know of this little nun who entered here with no dowry or curriculum vitae? She claims to be amnesiac. And our Mother Anthony of Padua, Superior of the convent at the time, was most imprudent to admit that girl into our holy house without any references.

Mother Marie-Clotilde immediately composes a long letter addressed to Mother Anthony of Padua, Superior of a convent lost in the backlands, in Lotbinière county, concerning Sister Julie.

While waiting for a reply, Mother Marie-Clotilde elaborates plans for getting rid of Sister Julie in the most discreet fashion.

"Let her go back to the world, this cross of my directorship, deprived of salvation like the world she never should have left. Is it not better that one of my daughters perish and that all the others be saved?"

Days go by.

Already, Sister Julie lives apart from the community. Cut off from her sisters like a rotten branch, deprived of mass and sacraments (she doesn't complain of this in the least), forgotten by all, by God and the devil, shut up in an enamel closet as in a toilet cell; she does not protest. One might think she were doomed to boredom, seemingly awaiting the end. In reality, Sister Julie is hoping for a letter.

This truce, this sudden peace, are undoubtedly Sister Gemma's gifts to us. Livid, blue, see how she suffers the convent's tribulations to the dregs. Her cut, burned hands, her ankles swollen by so much standing, stirring our daily gruels, can take no more. Her delicate nostrils catch the aroma of stale meat in the cold storage rooms. While the bitter smell of crimes committed in the house burns her nose and throat.

For several days now, she has been unable to take any nourishment. A mere drop of water turns her stomach. All contact injures her, to such an extent that they are afraid of hastening her death if they touch her with their fingertips.

They wrap her in immaculate bandages. They change her bedsheets twice a day. She obstinately refuses to see a doctor. She finds the very thought of a masculine presence leaning over her sickbed intolerable. The chaplain himself seems to her a bearer of dangerous germs. More than anything in the world she fears that the priest's hands, when she takes communion, might brush her mouth and make her pregnant. Adolescent memories come out of hiding. "Lascivious kisses" on the mouth, is it not thus that children, fruit of sin, are conceived? Refuse the succour of religion. Anything to avoid earthly promiscuity. Turn irremediably towards heaven. Die of starvation. Neither food nor eucharist. O! Heaven will deliver me of this corpse's body! Don't touch anything. Die, empty and hollow like an earthenware jar, awaiting God's fire, ravaging at will, annihilating her right down to the last fragment of her being.

Our little Sister Gemma is dying. Let us take care not to interfere with her desire to die. This desire is holy: it can come from God alone. Let us content ourselves with bringing her white roses. She'll not eat or drink or take communion if such is God's will! A little time yet and all will be consummated. Let us prepare a white cloth to wipe the last tear from her cheek, the last drop of sweat from her forehead. We will make relics of them.

The Sisters of the Precious Blood, after three hundred years of contemplative life in the shadow of a stone convent in the city of Quebec, will publicly produce a saint, and her glory will be reflected on the entire community, will save it from the bankruptcy caused by the Sister Bursar. None will then remember the devil's last onslaught against our holy community, for an instant in mortal danger but saved in the nick of time by Sister Gemma, who is dying her gentle death in the whiteness of her immaculate sheets.

The chaplain promises to administer extreme unction to Sister Gemma as soon as she becomes too weak to protest. He is posted at the infirmary door, dressed in his starched surplice and violet stole, a little black bag containing the holy chrism, the cotton and holy water in his hand. Awaiting Sister Gemma's end.

As for Doctor Painchaud, it has been several weeks

since he's set foot in the convent. We'll call him at the end to certify the death and sign the burial permit.

The time of waiting drags through the entire convent. The Rule is rigorously observed. Religious exercises and domestic duties are accomplished in an orderly way. There is an extraordinary silence. The shadow of death glides over us, chills and delights us.

The nursing sister, her penitence completed, has taken up vigil at Sister Gemma's side.

One morning she notices a few small drops of blood on the patient's lips. While she sleeps very peacefully, a vague smile on her pale face.

Wednesday morning of autumn Ember week. Blood gushes from Sister Gemma's mouth, runs down her chin and throat, stains her shirt. Sister Gemma seems miraculously rested. For the first time in weeks she is able to sit up in bed without help.

Saturday of Ember week. Mass is celebrated in the night of Saturday to Sunday. The thin song of the nuns rises beneath the gold and azure vaulting.

We beseech Thee almighty God

You sing with angelic voices, my Sisters, as if ignorant of all that concerns the depths and darkness of this convent. How well do you know the great kitchen saturated with the stink of greasy cabbage at the stroke of midnight? Have you ever prodded the mysterious shadows of its nooks crammed with strange and noisy utensils? Are you familiar with the narrow corridor leading to it, broken by stairs and every other kind of trap? The thick, heavy door of the cold cellar, so hard to push — it resists, groans on its hinges; it can close on you forever, freeze you to the bone like little turds. Unless you place a log there to keep it ajar and prevent its slamming shut on you.

The ancient anguish of raw-boned nocturnal beasts on the stalk for prey and blood. Their cunning, their elastic gait, their hollow growling. Two nuns slip into the cold storage room at that very instant.

The treasure of the salting tubs, the smoked hams hanging from beams, frozen chickens, yellow and grainy, immense quarters of beef on hooks, disemboweled rabbits with purple kidneys, come to life and redden like fresh sores under the flashlight's beam. The cellar is full of blood-red and yellow gleams that glow and die like firebrands.

Sister Gemma's bright eyes don't blink. Twice an attentive companion passes a light under her nose to ensure that she is deeply asleep.

Hatchet, slicer, bonesaw aren't too much to hew a substantial notch in the enormous frozen piece of beef.

"Let it thaw between your thighs all night, Sister. And tomorrow morning you'll have a real feast before the nurse comes to wake you with her thermometer and basin."

Sister Julie's laugh breaks out and resounds, savage and sonorous, in the frozen air.

Next morning the nursing sister discovers Sister Gemma stupid and lost, as if coming out of profound inebriety. She is sitting on the edge of the bed, legs dangling, her spread thighs dripping with blood. She is chewing with difficulty on a mouthful of raw meat, passing it from one side of her toothless mouth to the other.

Sister Gemma jabbers in a listless voice: she would like to wash and change her shirt. She also insists that she be given back her false teeth, which have been taken away from her as from the dying.

Sister Julie's prison is double-locked. And the key is still at the bottom of Mother Marie-Clotilde's pocket on a small ring. Yet it is in Sister Julie's room that they discover the blood-stained hatchet and knives shortly afterwards.

Sister Julie's treacherous, satisfied smile illuminates her from head to foot. She is standing in the middle of the room. Stark naked. Smeared with blood.

Sister Gemma begs them to lash her to her deathbed so that she will not commit any other mortal sin in her dreams. So she will never again wake in the morning to find her mouth full of raw meat and new life.

"It's as though the devil himself had given me communion in my sleep. Protect me, my Sisters! I want to die of starvation, to be nothing more than a light transparent soul, a white bird, a dove . . ."

"Your exalted notions will be your damnation, Sister. And you'll drag the entire convent down with you. He who tries to play the angel plays the beast, and you've proved it indeed, devouring raw meat in secret at night like a wild beast."

We'll stuff her with porridge, vegetable soup and blanc mange. We'll set her back on her flat feet and send her off to the linen room to sew buttons and do invisible mending. Let her be silent! Step aside! Disappear from our sight! May tribulation weigh heavy on her once again! We are going to measure her resistance and reckon her patience. Perhaps Sister Gemma will be all the greater for this new trial? Perhaps one day we will have our gentle anaemic saint, our shower of roses at last?

Léo-Z. Flageole warns the Superior against dangerous daydreams.

"That is nothing but pride, Mother. Be on your guard. Imposture lies in wait for all of us, like a bird of prey. Satan is toying with us. He leaves no stone unturned. Let us rather solemnly recite the prayer written by Pope Leo XIII that we may be delivered up from Satan's snares and illusions."

The entire community is assembled in the chapel, nuns crowded up against each other in one single vigilance, a single shiver of fear.

Léo-Z. Flageole's clear firm voice detaches each syllable.

O Glorious St. Michael, Prince of the heavenly host and Protector of the Universal Church, defend us against all our enemies visible and invisible, and protect us from their cruel tyranny; preserve us also from all spiritual and temporal dangers . . .

Father Flageole is unable to complete the prayer. An invincible force grips his throat and chest, devastates and chokes him, blocks all his bronchial and pulmonary outlets, sucking the air from them, seeking Léo-Z. Flageole's heart to break it. Mortal silence. Heart failure. Then the living-machine starts up again in the rib cage. Bellows of the forge. A squawky, wheezing, rattling accordion. The chaplain's aged ribs creak like a ship in a storm.

Léo-Z. Flageole is unable to utter a single word for several days. Sitting straight up in his bed, leaning on a pile of pillows, busy seeking vital air, he writes short notes to Mother Marie-Clotilde in a trembling hand.

"I try to catch my breath with each second. You must

write to the archdiocese, inform them of what's going on here as soon as possible. All this evil comes from Sister Julie. Exorcise her without delay. Watch over her day and night. Observe her without respite. Tell the Sisters who guard Sister Julie not to look her in the eye. Have them also carefully examine her hands, feet, belly and chest every day in order to detect all possible signs or stigmata. We must beware of any unusual symptoms. Pray, reverend Mother, that I may not suffocate to death — these asthma attacks are as violent as hellborn fury. I expect you to write to the archdiocese. I will sign the letter myself if God gives me the strength to do so.

LEO-Z. FLAGEOLE, P.S.

Three important letters marked *urgent* have gone out from the convent of the ladies of the Precious Blood. All three signed by Father Flageole, Mother Marie-Clotilde and her assistant. One addressed to the archdiocese, another to the Mother Provincial, and the first, sent several weeks ago already, to Mother Anthony of Padua in Lotbinière county.

You might just as well throw bottles in the ocean. There is a hitch somewhere in the mail service (unless it is in the very air we breathe); it prevents us from answering letters or taking action, delivers us up to a torpor propitious to perverse enchantments.

Mother Marie-Clotilde admits that Satan's presence bothers her less than the absence of God.

I, Julie of the Trinity, sleep all day, settled in my hospital bed like a fetus, knees up to my chin. It is thus that I can go back in time to the far-removed day when the waters covered the earth. My mother speaks to me through a pool. Telling me I possess powers that must be put to use.

I lift my head. Half open my snake eyes. I glimpse the two unmoving nuns watching over me, while they recite their rosary.

In an instant I will make my brother Joseph appear to

them standing in a corner of the room. More naked than Christ on the cross. Undoubtedly too handsome to be a man. His entire body stretched from head to toe like a rising flame. Immense transparent eyes, extremely pale. Long black lashes. Black curly hair. Strong white teeth (like mine, given to us by Philomène and Adélard). Silken skin. A smooth chest, two little copper nipples. A flat stomach. His fuzzy, fleecy tuft, only the slightest bit wiry. His penis, sweeter and gentler than any earthly sweetness or tenderness, will nest in my belly as a host melts in the mouth. O, what a dream! Joseph laughs. He says he'll gladly do anything. But not that. Never. I laugh. I tell him he can very well do anything, but not that.

A white wedding in a salmon room.

Don't be frightened, Sisters. Before you dash out of the room mumbling prayers, look fearlessly upon what follows. The worst is over now that I've given you the vision of Joseph standing naked in a corner. Don't leave yet. The rest is only strange fraternal tenderness. I'll take you around the salmon room. And perhaps around the entire cottage that has been shut up for the winter if you like.

Joseph likes me to caress him and rock him in my arms. *He says he is a marvellous child to rock*. We sleep pressed close together in an enormous bed with a Simmons mattress and white sheets with salmon trim. The entire room of narrow planking is painted a shiny salmon colour. There are blue and green cretonne curtains at the windows. A colour picture of Loretta Young is pinned on the right wall. Have you noticed her hazy gaze, her silly look, her fleshy, bright red lips? And on the dresser, the little green and yellow porcelain donkey? Two baskets attached to his pack do as ashtrays. A maple leaf covers his right eye.

No, no, this is not the shanty. There will never be a shanty again. The shanty is dead. And one must go on living elsewhere, according to other laws, become angels. (Forget that ferns burn under my feet.)

The handsome youths chosen by God, unless it was by the Other, to stock Noah's ark. Don't be mistaken. The boy and girl are squatters. They haven't dared open the shutters. River water laps beneath the windows. Sometimes you hear a fish jump in the air and fall back into the calm water. In the winter you listen to the nails cracking with cold in the boards of the roof and walls. It's easy to find an unoccupied cottage in the winter and safely take refuge there. You only have to be careful not to overdo things as far as heating is concerned. Because of the chimney smoke that could betray the young couple shut up inside. There are piles of canned goods on the kitchen shelves and marvellous can openers in the drawers.

In the summer the girl and boy hide in the forest to spy on the owners of the cottages. All along the river, all summer long, well hidden in the bushes, they follow entire conversations or bits of sentences, murmurs and family storms. The cottage owners eat and drink copiously and frequently. They bathe in the river, uttering little cries, shut themselves up in the evening to chat and play cards. Their shadows pass by in the orange light of the windows.

The brother and sister drag their sleeping bag with them all summer long, sleeping under the stars, identified with the soil of the forest, camouflaged with earth and branches, covered with leaves, soaked with rain or sun. They feel the forest as they feel their own bodies. What a life it is! Fishing, hunting, hunted and pursued like game. In the village they call them the wild children. A reward is offered for their capture. So many cases of breaking and entering, so many thefts in the cottages. So many traps visited and looted in the forest in the fall, hares and rabbits taken from the snare and made to vanish by expert hands.

Joseph is the first to be be caught. It was bound to happen. He's too fond of scouring around near the village. The church especially attracts and dazzles him. He swoons at the odour of candles and incense. When the priest in the pulpit pronounces the word "sin" he plunges into an abyss of reflection and terrible ecstasies. He especially likes it when the priest gives a sermon about the end of the world. The division of the good from the evil enchants him. He vows to be on the side of the just, swears he'll lead his sister along the road to righteousness.

In the evening he drinks beer found in unknown refrigerators with his sister, who is a filcher like himself.

Joseph praises the beauty of the religious ceremonies, the liturgy, the holy vessels, the sacerdotal ornaments, the holy water, the holy chrism of salvation, the rosary beads of black wood or coloured glass, the signs of the cross, the genuflections, the Latin, the Gregorian chants, the calm of the celebrant and his assistants. In a word, nothing to recall the ceremonies of the mountain of B . . . And yet it's the same weightless departure from oneself, the same flight towards strange raptures. Touching upon the life beyond, but in this case through gentleness and goodness. Joseph always harks back to the goodness. His eyes moisten when he talks about it. He says he was born in an evil world. Of those around him only his sister Julie might have become truly good and holy if she had wanted to take the trouble, even though she'd been initiated at an early age and completely perverted by . . .

He cries and blows his nose into his fingers.

The deadly softness of tears. See how the girl yields: she kneels at her brother's feet, implores him to love her always and bless her, lowers her head while he places a string bearing the medal of the Immaculate Conception around her neck.

So great is Joseph's charm that, cord on her neck, Julie can only give in to the rival magic her brother preaches. (Or pretend to give in.) Become an angel with him. For him. (Or pretend to become an angel.) Become a convert. Drive the merry devil that serves as her heart out from between her ribs.

Home life is strange and subdued. The brother and sister now avoid passing too close to one another.

Julie seems to be watching Joseph from a greater distance. Like certain birds (she possesses their very privilege) she can draw translucent eyelids over her copper eyes. Julie becomes aloof and seraphic at will. Her skin gleams no more than a lamp that's been turned off. At night she sleeps dressed in an old pair of men's pyjamas she found in a dresser drawer. Joseph falls asleep with his head on Julie's shoulder. In his dreams he chews the blue striped cotton of the pyjamas.

My darling little boy, my sweet little Christ-child! Be reassured. I am your foster sister, you bed sister, your sister of mercy. Sleep in peace! I'm only stroking your skin all over (for your good and mine) with my fingertips and lips. From the roots of your hair down to your toenails.

Joseph leaps from the warmth of the bed, rushes outside. I hear him moaning on the porch.

He comes back in to call me a damned witch and curls up on the floor near the front door. He swears he will never be "initiated"; not by Philomène, not by me, not by any other woman.

"No bloody witch will take me alive!"

He starts crying again. He spends the whole night on the floor, far from me. I also cry, alone in the big bed with pink sheets.

When I open my eyes in the morning Joseph is no longer there.

He comes back three days and three nights later. Shorn and scrubbed, disinfected, dressed as a soldier. A suffocating odour of Lifebuoy soap and quartermaster's stores shrouds him from head to toe.

The recruiting sergeant promised him that in the army they'd teach him to read and write, teach him English, and the Roman Catholic religion to boot. But the most extraordinary thing of all is that for a dollar and thirty cents a day they've asked Joseph to go fight the devil in the old countries.

"On the other side of the river is where. His name's Hitler. Seems he's putting everything to fire and sword over there. They say he's the Antichrist."

Even though I'm not really sure that the devil isn't still on this side of the river (hidden in a dark corner of the mountain of B . . .) I've accepted to betray him and renounce him completely, so that no harm will come to Joseph over in the old countries.

"Any person, in case of necessity, can and should perform baptism."

Suiting the action to his words, Joseph baptizes me in the river. I lower my head and study the pebbles at the bottom of the water, seen as through a very clear green oil.

"I baptize you in the name of the Father, the Son, and the Holy Ghost."

For a long while Joseph holds my head under water, until I choke.

"For your sins, my beauty, for mine and those of the whole world."

One woman constitutes this gaunt boy's entire family. Spouse, mother, fiancée, grandmother and cousin. I am all these at once. Joseph swears there will never be any other in his heart, but that I'll consequently have to pay the price as long as the war lasts.

I will be the total woman, the total victim, the guardian angel, the tutelary sister. Knit. Pray. Sacrifice myself for ten, for a hundred. In place of all the women he does not know (and should know), with their hidden love and their eternal khaki woolen knitting in their hands.

Joseph's gaze lingers in the distance, looking like the pebbles at the bottom of the river: misted with olive liquid, yet hard, opaque and grey.

In the office of Mother Marie-Clotilde of the Cross, Superior of the ladies of the Precious Blood.

"No, no, Mother, it wasn't Christ! Nor Saint Sebastian pierced with arrows. There was absolutely no cloth at all around his belly. He was completely naked. The wall behind him was salmon-coloured. Like a sunset or a fire gleaming."

"Sister Julie made him appear on the wall, him and the pink glow."

"Then she made him disappear with a wave of her hand."

"She fondled him."

"She kissed him."

"Even after he'd disappeared she carried on as though he was still there, invisible but present."

"I think she was talking to him."

"You couldn't hear what she was saying but you could

clearly see her lips move."

"Her hands, arms and feet were moving too."

"You got the feeling she was living an extraordinary life elsewhere."

"The motion of bringing a piece of bread to her lips."

"Of drinking."

"Of dressing and undressing."

"Going up and down stairs."

"Crying and laughing."

"Without any sound or real tears in her eyes."

"A kind of grimacing."

"Her eyes stayed fixed like those of a sleepwalker."

"Sister Ignatius of Loyola saw it all as I did."

"It's true, Mother, I was keeping watch on Sister Julie with Sister John Chrysostomus. I saw everything with her, as she saw it."

"We were absolutely incapable of moving or even lowering our eyes."

"We were frightened to death, but we were both frozen with fear, Mother, and with something more frightening than fear. With pleasure, ghastly pleasure brought about by the spectre's shameful beauty."

"Mother, I confess that I've known no happier moment in my life since my first communion."

"You wretched little creatures! The devil seduced you with Sister Julie's help! Get yourselves right off to confession, both of you, and pray to Saint Michael that he may *defend you in battle, that you perish not in the dreadful judgement*.

Mother Marie-Clotilde finished her sentence in solemn tones, reading from her missal the alleluia of the September 29th mass, dedicated to Saint Michael the Archangel.

Gusts of wind shake the convent framework and dash against the heavy bolted doors. In the sisters' little garden trees are twisted and shaken. Windows fly open here and there under the violent thrusts of air, to flap recklessly while the little nuns run from one floor to the other closing them again. Almost everywhere, in the refectory, wardrobe, study and meeting rooms, in the kitchen, washroom, sacristy, even in the chapel, objects are thrown to the ground, broken and shattered. Soon the rain, in heavy, resonant drops, lashes at the window panes.

Three in the afternoon. The sky is black as ink. Even before the first violet streak breaks through, Mother Marie-Clotilde, standing in her small, oak-wainscoted office, feels with surprising pain the absolute certitude that the convent is possessed. While the sisters, mouth pressed to ear, repeat in a murmur that the storm really began in the room where Sister Julie is held prisoner. When all was silent outside and in, didn't they hear the pharmacy jars roll on the ground and break as if responding to Sister Julie's furious wail upon learning that her brother's wife was pregnant? At that moment all was still calm in the city and in the sisters' garden. Surely too calm, as if petrified in the expectation of a catastrophe. But then, the mild temperature and thaw, completely unexpected in this season, had already plunged us into an abnormal state of prostration and langour.

"A thunderstorm! In the middle of January! It's unbelievable, Sister!"

Parce, Domine,
parce populo tuo:
ne in aeternum
irascaris nobis.

The Superior has sent all her able-bodied girls off to pray and sing in the chapel, in order to reassure and comfort them somewhat, and to attempt to stave off fate. While the storm and din coming from Sister Julie's room heighten in intensity and fury.

The morning mail brought a letter from the archdiocese along with a letter from Sister Julie's brother announcing that a blessed event . . .

In the letter from the archdiocese, the Grand Exorcist asks Father Flageole to telephone his secretary in order to explain certain details of Sister Julie's case.

She has not eaten or slept or relieved herself since yesterday. She even refuses to drink. That is what the two nuns charged with watching over her affirm.

A stepladder has been set in the corridor against Sister Julie's door. The two nuns, perched in turn on the top rung, carefully follow Sister Julie's doings and sayings through the transom window. An ingenious system composed of a pulley, ropes and small baskets has been contrived to provide for Sister Julie's wants and rid her of dirty dishes and chamber pots as they accumulate.

The two sisters on duty are in absolute agreement on this point. Even before the storm broke outside, the jars and vials piled up on the pharmacy shelves began flying in all directions through the room, as though flung about by a furious wind. They burst in flight then fell to the floor smashed to atoms.

There can no longer be any doubt about it: the epicentre of this mid-January tropical storm is indeed situated within the convent walls of the ladies of the Precious Blood, or more precisely in the pharmacy in which Sister Julie of the Trinity is imprisoned.

The rain quickly turns to freezing rain. The city is strewn with broken tree branches and all kinds of debris. The telephone and electricity have been cut off, due to lines snapped beneath the weight of the ice. An entire crystal city chinks in the wind like a shivered chandelier. A few indistinguishable creatures, their heads sunk down into their shoulders and arms clinging to their bodies, slip, flounder, run for shelter. Two of these creatures will be caught on their way by the voiceless call of Sister Julie, who stands at her window like a magnet. First Doctor Painchaud. Then Marilda Sansfaçon.

Ever since Léo-Z. Flageole noticed that the convent telephone was out, he finds it harder to breathe. Now he must act quickly and alone. The storm has put the help of the Grand Exorcist beyond his reach.

The chaplain dons the stole and violet cope. He has prepared the holy water and the exorcism ritual. Mother Marie-Clotilde has had holy candles lit in the corridor. A second stepladder is placed against the pharmacy door. The chaplain and Superior press their faces against the transom.

Sister Julie is treading on shards of broken bottles strewn about the floor. She seems to feel no pain, although her feet are scraped and bleeding.

Her movements are disordered. Cast alive into an invisible world, she relives in a few minutes her entire existence on the mountain of B . . .

"Joseph is an angel! He loves me like an angel!"

She gives a piercing shriek: "He betrayed me, the bastard!"

She tears her clothes and throws them on the floor, tramples them and draws marks all over her body and face with her own blood, mixed by the handful with the black ashes she takes from her felt scapulary, having torn it open with her teeth. She dances and writhes. She clamours that she's a red vixen and that the fox "by her odour enticed" wants to dance with her. She is so realistic, so convincing that the fox is present there, in the room with her, although you can't see him. She executes dance steps with the *Other*, opposite her, and mimes. Mother Marie-Clotilde and Léo-Z. Flageole hear the faint sound of claws tapping opposite Sister Julie. They follow Sister Julie in each of her rhythmical movements.

"It's a fox-trot, Sisters, banned as a mortal sin in the entire diocese of Quebec by the cardinal himself!"

She utters a strident cry.

"Watch out! They're going to be wed before your eyes! The two fox-trotters! Joseph and his Piggy-Wiggy English girl!"

Sister Julie turns about, shakes herself as if casting off a useless weight.

"Look now, reverends, how the Piggy shakes her Joseph of a husband, and not without reason . . ."

She chokes with laughter. Now she sits on the floor amidst the broken bottles. She busies herself silently. You might think she was holding a long rope in her hands, making very tight knots in it. You can hear the hissing sound as it glides over her thighs.

Léo-Z. Flageole's suffocated voice puffs against Mother Marie-Clotilde's starched coif.

"The knotting of the aiguillette is an evil spell that prevents the bridegroom from administering the marriage sacrament to his bride. It's an abominable crime, condemned by all theologians. It's a good thing I'm here."

The chaplain sighs with pleasure, delightedly recalls the long nights spent huddled beside his study lamp, fine embroidery scissors in hand, contriving to undo one by one the numerous knots Sister Julie had accumulated on the hempen rope she wears as a belt, like all the other ladies of the Precious Blood.

He makes his entry now. Pulls Sister Julie's belt from his pocket. Sister John Chrysostomus had brought it to him at his request. Stole and violet cope. He throws the smooth rope, rid of its knots, at Sister Julie.

She jumps aside as if a snake had fallen at her feet. The chaplain's joy knows no bounds in the presence of this woman who fears him and his superior powers. Sister Julie is given a partner in her delirium. She turns against him, accepts him as an enemy, wants to destroy him immediately. Sister Julie's strong hands squeeze Léo-Z. Flageole's neck.

Mother Marie-Clotilde cries out for help, torn away from Sister Julie's act, which up to then she had been watching, fascinated, from the doorway.

Like a child casting off one toy for another, Sister Julie turns away from the half-asphyxiated chaplain while the Superior leads him away and double-locks the door.

Sister Julie is immediately filled with the death of Philomène, burned alive.

She struggles against fire and smoke, cries out, coughs and chokes. She is covered with sores and writhes in pain. A strange voice scoffs through her burned belly.

"The witch must die in despair. It's she! It's my mother. It is I. I am she and she is I. I'm burning! It's my turn now."

Sister Julie drags herself to the window, looks through the bars at something that cannot really be seen from the second floor. Sister Julie calls to something she does not see, something she knows is there on the sidewalk waiting to be called to inhabit with her the narrow space of her possession. On an equal footing.

Since the storm began Jean Painchaud has not been able to take his mind off Sister Julie of the Trinity, struggling as if he were in the middle of a tempest.

He leaves the hospital around five o'clock and proceeds towards the convent through gusts of wind, torrential rain and sleet. The steep, narrow streets are like skating rinks riddled with holes.

Neither the extern sister nor the Superior are to be seen. Not a single cornet flutters in the corridors. In the distance women's voices intone a psalm of penance, in the chapel. The doctor goes directly to the room in which Sister Julie has been kept prisoner for several months. He finds the key in the lock.

He speaks to her. She seems not to hear. He touches her eye with his finger. She doesn't blink. He sees her burns.

This creature is beyond reach, far beyond reach: entrenched inside herself, reduced to her very core, her narrowest self. Far from us all she lives a thousand lives and deaths.

The doctor wonders if some strong emotion imposed from outside her might not save Sister Julie, bring her back on solid ground, back to normal daily life. A life in which the love of an ordinary man like Jean Painchaud would be a gift from heaven. He leans over Sister Julie. Wanting to confess to her: he loves her like a lunatic and desires her like a man. In broad daylight. In actual reality. He shakes her by the shoulders to wake her.

"You must get out of this convent! You must! You must! Right away! Quick!"

Sister Julie eyes him from between her lashes. She begs him to approach her, to dress her wounds and breathe the breath of her distress close by her mouth. Her urgent voice is barely audible — thus moan the dead beneath the ground. She tells him that the direct contact of a healthy, compassionate skin alone can heal her wounds.

The doctor leans over Sister Julie. His big hands, cool and plump, become ever more feverish as they caress Sister Julie's afflicted body. At the limit of his strength, he feels all Sister Julie's sores as if they were his own. He gently glides into Sister Julie's hell with her. Never will he be able to bring that woman back to a habitable world. On the contrary it is she who will draw him down into the bottomless pit.

Here she is, superb and damned, even as she appears in the very depths of Jean Painchaud's nightmares. He has just enough strength to get up and back away towards the door. Two yellow eyes fixed upon him. A voice escapes from Sister Julie's belly to mock and scoff.

"Darling treasure of pious souls. I am Satan's mystical body. So are you. Both of us. You are damning yourself in my stead. I feel extremely well now. Thank you, dear heart."

Sister Julie stretches out white and smooth on her bed like a cat in the sun, suddenly healed. The doctor's hands are covered with suppurating blisters, like those caused by poison plants.

At the height of the storm Marilda Sansfaçon, drenched like an otter leaving the stream, sought refuge with the ladies of the Precious Blood.

The Superior, the assistant and the extern sister noticed nothing suspicious about the woman. Clothed in a black sealskin coat and black fur-trimmed boots, she had a long nose, little gold-rimmed glasses and pallid hands with red painted nails. About forty years old. She sat erect and stiff on one of the small parlour chairs, her knees pressed together. At first she kept pulling her coat flaps over them. She took her little glasses, fogged with rain and frost, from her nose, carefully wiped them, and set them back in place. She heaved a little sigh of relief and began to relax. She opened her coat. Her black satin dress is very short and slit up the side. Her umbrella has been turned inside-out. It drips on the floor, but this seems to bother nobody. She smells of tobacco, gin and cheap perfume.

Her voice is low, raucous, and very excited.

"Who is that standing in the window on the second floor of your damned convent? Who is looking down in the street, making me lift my head as I go by? Who's that calling me with a voice from beyond the grave, me, Marilda Sansfaçon?"

The short body is sunk into the chair, the interminable legs stretched out in the parlour aisle.

She loses the thread of her thoughts, begins coughing. She talks about the storm and the woman she saw in the window, as perfectly distinct in the thunder and lightning as in full daylight, her face all white, her back all white. Because the woman in the window was turning around like a top, bending down, rising, showing her head, or her behind flashing like lightning.

The woman in the sealskin coat weeps bitterly. She insists that the creature up there on the second floor looks like . . . who? Everyone knows she was shacked up with the devil and . . . in the old days, at Georgiana's she used to filch all her clients.

You should take that woman with tongs (not to dirty your hands) and get her back out on the street as quickly as you can. Yet Mother Marie-Clotilde questions her.

"Who do you mean, my daughter?"

"I'm not your daughter, thank God. I never had a mother, but I prefer that to . . ."

She laughs and chokes. Begins crying again.

"The most frightening part of it, Mother, is that the face of the creature up there in the window lit up all of a sudden like a firebrand and then went black as coal, just like the other one at Georgiana's — they say she was burned to death in her shanty."

Mother Marie-Clotilde's voice, ever more faltering, insists.

"Where was this shanty? In what region? What parish? Do you know, my daughter?"

"Somewhere in the country, out by . . I don't recall. Her

old man's name was Adélard, that I remember well . . . Adélard."

Adélard's name brings on a new fit of hilarity and coughing.

"You are drunk, my daughter, and you're seeing things."

"It is not the visions that crucify me most, reverend, it's not being able to remember names. But I'll find them out. I'm gonna come back here with all the information you want, when you want. I promise you."

"The door is this way, my daughter," says the extern sister, rattling her key ring.

"I'll come back another day with all the information. But that'll be five bucks for finding Adélard's name, Mother, cash."

A wanton woman was stabbed to death on Canoterie Hill Saturday night. The police have identified one of her soldier friends as a murder suspect. The man boarded ship in Halifax yesterday on his way to the front, somewhere in England.

The new cook of the ladies of the Precious Blood claims someone stole a sharp knife from the kitchen. It was found under Sister Julie's bed.

The carefully polished knifeblade shone brightly. Sister Julie's robe, with large wet patches, had been hung on a nail near the window to drip. Her brother's wedding picture is still pinned to the wall. The bride's belly is riddled with pins. The groom's left side torn by a knife.

If I can't place my fingers in the wound in his side, I shall not believe, moans Sister Julie. She rolls her head on the pillow. Begs some unyielding being in the shadow to stop the machinery that has already been set in motion on the other side of the Atlantic.

And now Sister Julie succeeds in drawing the far-off image of her brother to her, with the air and the place where he is still clinging to him, like a young tree uprooted with all its indispensable soil. There are shelves full of bottles and glasses in a row. A bit of counter shining bare and metallic. Black stools. You can hear a record playing slowly, running out of breath. There are two Sister Julies now. One is dancing with her brother, who is dressed as a soldier, and the other sees herself dancing with him, in a dark, deserted London pub. A mournful, unending, slow fox-trot.

Joseph lives, but his face is marked by such sadness that Sister Julie immediately understands that the first of his misfortunes has just taken place.

You must console this boy, be kind and gentle to him, infinitely compassionate. But the slightest gesture on Sister Julie's part can set off the rest of the history that has already been decided inside Joseph's very body, which is preparing and arranging itself to receive a bullet right in the heart, according to the foreseen plan.

He looked at me once. Just once. It's unbearable. He says his wife and child are already dead.

The sky is blue. Snow and ice sparkle in the bright sun. The air is mild. Not a breath of wind. City trucks come and go, clearing away fallen trees, branches and all kinds of debris piled up by the storm.

The electricity and telephone lines have been repaired since this morning. Once again the ladies of the Precious Blood are linked to the city.

A little telegraph boy brings news for Sister Julie. The telegram is signed: Joseph. He announces the death of Piggy and the child. For the second telegram, there'll be a wait until the battle of Cassino is well underway, and into its most murderous phase.

Piggy-Wiggy, see where it got you. You never should have done it, my lovely English piglet. Sister Julie is as jealous as a tigress. You shouldn't have defied her, taken away her only love, nor above all subjected Joseph to conjugal duty. Conceived in such deplorable conditions, it is only just that the nameless, unbaptized, stillborn child be cast back into Limbo, from which he should never have emerged.

Fortunately the savage joy that used to preside over Sister Julie's life persists in spite of religion and passing time. It keeps Sister Julie from being too moved by the death in childbirth of her sister-in-law and her child. Dispensed from mourning, she laughs openly in the face of Mother Marie-Clotilde when she comes to offer her condolences.

The Grand Exorcist has arrived, He asks to see the exhibits. Sister Julie's belt is carefully examined with a magnifying glass to detect the marks of the knots Father Flageole undid there. Two photographs hold particular interest for the Grand Exorcist. One of them, full of pinholes, represents a young bride and bridegroom. The other, clipped from a newspaper, shows the laughing, painted face of a woman. The caption says that she was murdered on Canoterie Hill.

"That woman had promised to bring us very precious information concerning Sister Julie's past."

Mother Marie-Clotilde is interrupted by Léo-Z. Flageole's wheezing voice.

"Sister Julie tried to strangle me during a fit of fury — me, chaplain of the convent, man of God and consecrated priest."

"You have attempted to deliver Sister Julie of the evil

that possesses her by all the ordinary means — prayer, fasting, penance, medicine?"

The Grand Exorcist's voice is calm and velvety, monotonous and slightly scornful.

He asks to see Sister Julie.

Coif, veil, cornet, wimple, barb, scapulary, she has piously donned the angelic formal vestments of her order. Which doesn't displease the Grand Exorcist, extremely sensitive to the beauty of religious costumes. She kneels at the feet of the Grand Exorcist and he hears her confession. She receives absolution and does penance, eyes lowered and hands tucked away in her wide sleeves.

Nothing but venial sins, convent trifles, thinks the Grand Exorcist. It's not worth shouting at the devil over it, but since the bishop has given the order we'll exorcise her, this lovely person, and the entire convent with her, Father Flageole in the lead, so that the wind of folly blowing in the house may die down.

The Grand Exorcist leafs with his right hand through the file drawn up by the chaplain in his crabbed, jerky handwriting. Sister Julie's spells are described in detail there. Enchantments, knotting of the aiguillette, the evil eye, her she-wolf's pupils, sores and stigmata, spells cast on the entire convent. The Grand Exorcist is bored. His left hand sadly pinches at the cloth of his cassock. Is not the greatest misfortune of the war the fact that it deprives the high clergy of those marvellous Italian cloths and the elegant cut of the Roman tailors?

The exorcism takes place with great pomp in the chapel in the presence of the entire community.

The Grand Exorcist, closely shaved, dressed in an Irish lace cassock and violet stole, places a second stole (of a more common cloth) on Sister Julie's shoulders while she holds a candle in her hand. She is then copiously sprinkled with holy water and bathed in clouds of incense. Prayer follows prayer. The entire community recites the litanies of the saints, intones the *Veni Creator Spiritus*.

The Grand Exorcist places his right hand on Sister Julie's head. She is kneeling. Another prayer. Then the Grand Exorcist makes the sign of the cross with his right thumb on Sister Julie's forehead, eyes, ears, nostrils and chest.

Signum crucis Christi, signum Salvatoris Domini nostri sit in fronte tua; ut confidas in eo.
Benedico oculos tuos ut videas claritatem ejus.
Benedico aures tuas, ut audias verbum veritatis.
Benedico nares tuas, ut recipias odorem suavitatis.
Benedico pectus tuum, ut credas in eum.
Benedico os tuum, ut confitearis illi, qui in Trinitate perfecta vivit et regnat Deus, per omnia saecula saeculorum.

"Amen," replies Sister Julie. At the light touches of the Grand Exorcist, like velvet paws, a gentle warmth penetrates her, makes her look like one of the blessed at her Saviour's feet. Yet it is from Sister Julie herself that an enchantment comes forth, to win over the Grand Exorcist to his immediate delight. Every time he gives Sister Julie unction it seems to him that the soft opulence of the most beautiful, the finest cloths of Europe, America, Africa and Asia pass under his delicate fingers. As if Sister Julie (finally rid of her eternal soul and her corpse's body) had been suddenly changed into a bolt of sumptuous cloth.

The Grand Exorcist is grateful to Sister Julie. He can thus avoid all physical contact, so trying for exorcist's fingers, during the ceremony.

The Grand Exorcist dons his head-covering. He questions Sister Julie of the Trinity in French. He asks her, according to the ritual, what she has done and how she has behaved herself in the convent over the last few months.

In a voice the Grand Exorcist alone can hear, Sister Julie recites: "Advent has already begun for me, reverend. I am pregnant and don't quite know when I'll give birth. Get me out of the convent quickly, for scandal is drawing near."

The Grand Exorcist sprinkles holy water on Sister Julie. He places holy salt on her tongue.

Deum, qui te genuit, dereliquisti, et oblita es Domini Dei Creatoris tui.

Sister Julie brushes the Exorcist's fingers with her teeth and tongue as she tastes the salt.

Ipse tibi imperat, Diabole, qui ventis et mari, ac tempestatibus imperavit; Ipse tibi imperat, maledicte, qui te de supernis coelorum in inferiora terrae demergi praecepit; Ipse tibi imperat, qui Adam primum hominem clamavit! Ipse tibi imperat, qui Ananiam, Azariam, Mizaalem in camino ignis salvavit; ut recedas ab hac famula Dei. Audi ergo Satana, victus et prostratus recede; in nomine Patris, et Filii, et Spiritus sancti.

The Grand Exorcist is pale with disgust and fear. He hurries on:

Adest, inique Spiritus, judex tuus; adest summa potestas; jam resiste si potes. Adest ille, qui pro salute nostra passurus, nunc, inquit, princeps hujus mundi ejicietur foras. Hoc illud corpus est, quod de corpore Virginis sumptum est, quod in spiritu crucis extensum est, quod in tumulo jacuit, quod de morte surrexit, quod videntibus Discipulis ascendit in coelum. In hujus ergo majestatis terribili potestate, tibi Spiritus maligne, praecipio, ut ab hac creatura ejus egrediens, contingere eam deinceps non praesumas.

Once again the Grand Exorcist makes the sign of the cross on Sister Julie's forehead. But in reality he carefully avoids touching her, blessing her just closely enough to deceive. But Sister Julie knows and softly smiles.

Conjuro et contestor te, Diabole immunde, per nomen Domini nostri Jesu Christi, et imperium ejus, et per virtutem sanctae Trinitatis, per potentiam ejus; et tu, Satana exeas, et omnis tua diabolica virtus et potestas immunda ab hac christiana recedat absque laesione animae et corporis. Vade retro Satana.

Sister Gemma claims that each time Satan's name was pronounced during the ceremony a dirty, stinking little angel three or four inches high with sparrow's wings and a red dress would jump up and down in the lower left side of the chapel, as if driven from its usual shelter and suddenly obliged to flee in great haste.

As for the Grand Exorcist, he didn't breathe a word of Sister Julie's extraordinary secret to the religious authorities.

He finds his silence inexplicable.

I'm an accomplice, I'm sure I'm an accomplice.

Back in his room he washed and scrubbed his hands endlessly in his desire to purify himself of Sister Julie's rough tongue and white teeth. At the same time the Grand Exorcist seemed to await some unknown favour secretly promised by Sister Julie during the ceremony.

He was not overly surprised to see Sister Julie appear in his room that very night.

She carried a purple velvet sack with gold fringes, made from an old door curtain, on her back.

"Cardinal's purple, little daddy! That's it! Look, touch, listen, feel how good it is. You could eat it."

In a second the Grand Exorcist's bed was strewn with splendid vestments and sumptuous insignia. Moiré copes, fine lace surplices, embroidered chasubles, golden crozier, amethyst ring and bishop's mitre.

Until morning, Sister Julie changed the Grand Exorcist into what he really was: puerile, frivolous and vain. He lounged among the beautiful clothes, caressed them, tried them on. Paraded before the mirror in great pomp.

The enchantment lasted until the Angelus rang in the belfry of the basilica.

The Grand Exorcist had a hard time arousing himself from sleep that morning. His eyelids were heavy and he was filled with nausea.

If it's a girl I'll call her my little pussycat, my owl. If it's a boy I'll call him my love. I'll succeed where poor Piggy failed. Shut up in a convent, I'll give birth by magic. Once he's born I'll make my son sleep between my thighs until he is mature, until he becomes a man. I will triumph where Philomène failed. I will lie with my son. Such is the ancient law. The greatest sorcerer is he who . . . I, Julie Labrosse called of the Trinity, I will do that. I will be mother and grandmother, mistress and witch, I'll experience anew the deepest law graven in my bones. I'll forget this convent and its pitiful magic, I'll forget the whole sickly Church and my brother Joseph who betrayed me. He has rightly been condemned to death. But we must await the last days, the most barbarous moments of the long battle of Cassino, before his heart bursts in his chest. Just a few more months to wait, my little Joseph, before you can die. Not in peace but in horror. Count on my

Medusa's head bent over you at the last moment. If only you recognize me my sorrows will be requited. And to cap it all, if I have time, I will even be able to announce to you the blessed event taking place in my nun's belly . . .

She has no more periods. She vomits all she eats as she swallows it. She demands corn, red currants, viburnum and cranberry jelly — all kinds of food you don't find in the convent. She drools like a child cutting teeth. She is constipated. She pees once an hour to the great annoyance of the sister charged with hauling the baskets back through the transom over her door. But she spends most of her time sleeping, arms and legs spread, struck down in a blissful stupour. On wakening she opens her shirt and gravely weighs her breasts, calls one of the guardian sisters to verify with her the swelling volume of her taut, heavy breasts. Her nipples are harder and more sensitive. When she touches them with her fingertips Sister Julie utters little cries of pleasure and pain. Certain smells have become unbearable to her. Incense and cabbage send her writhing with disgust on her bed.

The sisters watching over her strictly observe the order

to keep silence, but everybody knows what is going on. Sister Julie is locked in, but she sends out waves that are propagated through the entire house. She is the centre of life and exists so intensely among the living dead that it becomes unbearable. She proclaims she is pregnant and that she is going to live her pregnancy out to the very end in sound and fury.

Jean Painchaud, in spite of his vow never to set foot in the convent again, examines Sister Julie. He asks her precise questions. He is more like a touchy, suspicious husband than a doctor.

The doctor is immensely interested in Sister Julie's breasts. Is he not the only one to see the little bumps surrounding the areolas?

He comes back day after day, fascinated by what is happening in Sister Julie's body. Each time he questions her at length, while the Superior watches. But it is only after four months have passed that he obtains Mother Marie-Clotilde's permission to practise a complete gynecological examination.

Tiny brown spots cover Sister Julie's face, so close together as to become an earthy mask. Her eyes seem paler, suddenly stripped of their pupils, liquid as puddles. The median line of her belly is brown and seems to have been drawn with a brush. A kind of whitish liquid flows from her swollen breasts. The uterus has grown considerably larger.

And yet Doctor Painchaud cannot detect the child's heartbeat with his stethoscope. Sister Julie claims her child loathes strangers. He curls up in his lodgings and stops his heartbeat as soon as he is auscultated. No use insisting: the child might fall into a syncope.

"Anyway I don't think my child has a heart!"

She laughs.

With the Superior the doctor speaks of an imaginary pregnancy. But he takes care not to admit what he alone knows. Sister Julie is not a virgin. This knowledge brings an almost unbearable twinge to Jean Painchaud's heart.

My child lives. My child is stirring. He kicks me in the liver. My child has no father. He is mine and mine alone. I have this power. Adélard and Philomène conferred it upon me when they anointed me witch and all-powerful on the mountain of B . . .

A crown on my head, my hands and feet bound, they take me in their arms and carry me around the chalk circle drawn on the floor. They call the masters of the North, East, South and West in low voices. Wind begins to whistle around the shanty. I swear to obey the law.

Two nuns' faces, their noses crushed against the transom. Their testimony is irrefutable.

"Sister Julie became stiff as a board. Her ankles and wrists looked as if they were attached with cords."

"Her whole taut body rose up above the bed without support. You would have thought she was floating on air."

"Her head was thrust backwards like a dead person's."

"It became very cold in the corridor. A strong draught shook the stepladder on which we, Sister Julie's guardians, were both perched."

The transom window has been whitewashed and the two guardians sent off to the chapel at the Superior's command. Mother Marie-Clotilde will personally take care of everything concerning service to Sister Julie.

Now Léo-Z. Flageole accompanies the Superior into Sister Julie's lair. He studies her attentively, takes notes, prepares a second more voluminous file for the archdiocese.

A letter arrives from Lotbinière county at last. Mother Anthony of Padua had begun the letter addressed to Mother Marie-Clotilde as follows:

"I first met Sister Julie of the Trinity when she entered our holy house. She must have been about thirteen or fourteen years old. She had lice, and the mange, and our first task was to wash and care for her. Her piety was remarkable. Her love of penance stupefying. Although she could neither read or write she acquired both skills in just a few weeks' time. As for her family, I find myself obliged to . . ."

Stricken with a heart attack, Mother Anthony of Padua never did finish the letter.

Jean Painchaud pines for Sister Julie. There are no more spectres in the doctor's office at night. No anguish, no voluptuousness. Doctor Painchaud rediscovers his boring monotonous life as it was before Sister Julie's time. Only the thought of Sister Julie's pregnancy stirs him out of boredom and gives him life, chagrin and jealousy.

Like a furious little monkey, Sister Julie's brown face puckers, grimaces, enters a trance. She flails her arms about, struts and sways, taps her feet, spits and grinds her teeth. She scratches herself until her whole body bleeds, seemingly searching her hair for fleas and crushing them between the nails of her thumb and index finger. You can hear something crack between her fingers. All around her you hear tiny sounds like heavy, spaced-out raindrops falling on the floor. She arches her back and pushes out her enormous belly streaked with delicate little rose and pearly lines.

"Darling treasure of pious souls, listen carefully. You hear all that kicking around in there? It's my darling baby breaking loose."

Sister Julie's taut belly is shaken by convulsions and contractions.

The doctor lets his stethoscope fall. He takes hold of Sister Julie's wrist, mumbles so that neither the Superior nor the chaplain hears what he says.

"Who is the father of the little monster tossing about in there?"

Sister Julie's laugh is so throaty and violent that the doctor recoils. She collapses with laughter on the bed.

"Damn you! Damn you!" screams the doctor.

He goes out and slams the door. He won't be back for a week.

On Léo-Z. Flageole's order Mother Marie-Clotilde has gone out of her convent. Now she trots along Saint Jean Street. She hugs the walls, her gaze lowered to the ankles of those who pass her. She enters Woolworth's with precaution and purchases a dozen packages of *Milwards Needles Nickel Plated*.

Sister Julie has been tied to her bed in her sleep. Léo-Z. Flageole is feverish and out of breath. He gives orders to Mother Marie-Clotilde. Hands her the soap and shaving-brush, then the razor. The Superior prays to God that she may not vomit before it's done. The chaplain prays to God that the *stigma diaboli* may be clearly located on Sister Julie's body.

Hair shorn, eyebrows, armpits and pubis shaved, Sister Julie spits like an angry cat.

Mother Marie-Clotilde is thorough and persevering. She pricks Sister Julie's entire body with needles, seeking the compromising mark of insensitivity under Léo-Z. Flageole's direction. The devil eludes her. Hours go by. Sister Julie's flesh reacts normally, suffers and bleeds when pricked.

Far into the night, when the breathing of victim and torturers has melted into one, harrowing and forced, the magic mark is discovered on Sister Julie's lower back and left shoulder. No sensitivity. Not a drop of blood. Just clear, pearly scars that testify to old wounds.

Mother Marie-Clotilde is afraid she'll faint. She takes off her glasses and wipes her forehead. Her wild mare's eyes seem about to burst their sockets.

Léo-Z. Flageole has been miraculously cured of his asthma. Calm and rested, he works on his report for the archdiocese until late morning, having forgotten to say mass.

She, always she, rising without cease from her ashes from generation to generation, from one pyre-stake to another. Herself mortal and palpable yet supernatural and maleficent: her flesh and bones, her treacherous smile, her teeth, her nails and bones . . . Her shorn hair grows back like the hair of the dead. (Six feet down, the wispy, vivacious growth on the white skull.) She, whom you imprison only to see her slip away through the walls like water or air. She is everywhere at once. Now in the pharmacy where they keep her prisoner among the ladies of the Precious Blood, or on Canoterie Hill, where an old prostitute was stabbed to death, or at her sister-in-law's side while she gives birth. *Somewhere in England*. Mother and child are poorly, die together. Sister Anthony of Padua was unable to finish her letter. Sister Julie's evil eye fixed itself on the old nun who knew too much. She, pregnant with I know not what sacrilegious fetus. Man or devil, it's an abomination. She, in blasphemy and filth. She, day and night acting like some rotten yeast upon the souls of her defenceless companions in this convent. She: always she! A witch! And her mother was one too. (Everyone knows that sorcery is hereditary.) And her great-grandmother. And her great-great-grandmother. And the ancestor back there at the beginning of the line. She crosses the ocean in a sailing ship in the middle of the seventeenth century. She, with whom her husband never could "get on" over in the old country, in France, because she was a witch. She slips among the immigrants and sets foot in Canada. She tames wild herbs mixed with the forest undergrowth. She prepares unguents and drugs, decants hate and love, drives them mad, leaves them all coupled together, knotted alive, in the new lands.

I, Léo-Z. Flageole, priest and chaplain of the ladies of the Precious Blood, solemnly swear, on this third day of January 1944, that Sister Julie of the Trinity is a sorceress, bearing the sign of the devil on her body in two different places. On her lower back and left shoulder. Sister Julie received this lamentable condition from her mother, who had it from her grandmother, and so on back up to Barbe

Hallé, born in La Coudray, Beauce, France, in 1645.

Ever since they practised the operation of the needles on Sister Julie's body Mother Marie-Clotilde has not been able to sleep. She roams about the convent all night long in the formal costume of the ladies of the Precious Blood. The slightest sigh in the shadows attracts her and sets her running from one end of the convent to the other. She comforts the sick, soothes the novice crying in her pillow, listens at great length with her ear pressed to doors, desperately wanting to erase everything. To repair everything. To prevent sorrow from taking root and spreading through the entire convent like an encroaching plant.

One night a continuous far-off wail, crying endlessly with a single breath, brings Mother Marie-Clotilde to the attic.

There is a little black iron bed in a corner of the attic. A child lies on his back with a white blanket pulled up to his chin. He cries on a single tone without beginning or end. But is it really a child? Mother Marie-Clotilde draws closer and bends over the bed. She sees despair close up with her pitiless, nearsighted eyes.

"Eternal damnation," thinks Mother Marie-Clotilde. She looks. She cannot help looking, although the sight is more unbearable than any vision of Christ crucified. A body, half-child, half-beast, tortured through all eternity. The tiny head of a kid, its horns filed down.

Mother Marie-Clotilde knows she is in the presence of Satan, yet she cannot help feeling great compassion.

Next morning there is no sign of the iron bed in the attic.

Let us pray my Sisters.

Kyrie eleison
Christe eleison

"Her child is growing every day."
"She really pushes it out."
"She must feel it right up under her ribs. He bothers her breathing. He bothers her swallowing."
"He takes up all the room inside."

Holy Mary,
Holy Virgin of virgins,
Mother of divine grace,

"It must be a boy. His heart beats like a drum, resounds all through the room where they keep her. I heard it on the other side of the closed door when I was going by in the corridor."

Seat of wisdom,
Cause of our joy,

"Mother Marie-Clotilde covered the window over Sister Julie's door with white paint. I scratched a little corner clear with a broomstick. I pulled a stepladder up . . ."

Mystical Rose,
Tower of David,
Tower of ivory,

"The doctor doesn't dare use his stethoscope anymore. She has forbidden it."

"She claims it might make her baby die. How sadly the doctor looks at Sister Julie!"

"She has no need of the doctor's pity."

House of gold,
Ark of the Covenant,
Gate of Heaven,

"The doctor was angry at Sister Julie. He accused her of play-acting. He says her big belly is empty and full of air like a balloon."

Morning Star,
Health of the sick,
Refuge of sinners,

"My God, what a miracle? What a dream! Why Sister Julie? Why not me?"

"Or me?"

"Or me? That child, she made it herself, without the help of any man."

"You know very well that isn't possible, Sister."

"The Virgin Mary managed to do it."

"Only once in the entire history of mankind, one virgin mother."

"What if the Messiah tried to come back on earth?"

"What if it's the Antichrist?"

"Stop it, Sisters, you're killing me."

"I say it's the devil who . . . Sister Julie is possessed."

"Unless she sinned with the doctor."

"That's not possible. Our Mother Superior always accompanies the doctor into Sister Julie's room."

"It would be a great crime."

"A mortal sin, Sister."

Lamb of God, Who takest away the sins of the world,
Spare us, O Lord.

"I thought I heard a child cry out. Don't you hear it, Sister?"

It was a tiny cry that seemed far off, as if shut up inside walls, hardly a second ago. You can't tell if you dreamed it or not. It was like a little lost kitten.

Lamb of God, Who takest away the sins of the world,
Hear us, O Lord.

Silence.

Orders are to pray unceasingly. One litany after the other! It is late. Orders are not to budge from the chapel. Orders are to cut off all communication with the outside world. No visitor can now be admitted to the parlour of the ladies of the Precious Blood.

"I am the lady of the most precious blood!" shouts Sister Julie'

She is sitting on the edge of the bed. Her spread legs streaming with blood. She holds a newborn baby in her arms. Licks it, breathes into its mouth. She is triumphant.

Three people have rushed into the room as if entering the cage of a lioness who'd just whelped.

Sister Julie springs to her feet, the child in the crook of her arm. She picks up something and puts it in her mouth. She says it's her child's placenta, that she must swallow it for her own good. She shows her teeth.

"I chewed the cord to cut it!"

In a room hardly bigger than a closet Mother Marie-Clotilde, Father Flageole and Doctor Painchaud breathe the same poisoned air as Sister Julie. Shut in with her, delivered up to the same spells, they are there, stupefied. Facing an inconceivable situation.

How can it be possible? This girl — guarded, watched, cooped up in a double-locked convent — managed to have a baby! By magic, she says. And now we have a baby on our hands, we, the ladies of the Precious Blood! Scandal breeds scandal. Soon we will live by the same laws as Sister Julie. One single mad reality for all. One single total wickedness. Solicited by the devil, we will respond to him and be moved by him in our turn. Cruelty will hold no more secrets for us.

Save the convent's reputation at any price!

Léo-Z. Flageole and Mother Marie-Clotilde have not exchanged a single word or look, yet they have already decided on their integration into Sister Julie's world. The child's fate is sealed for the peace of the convent. When evil is let loose it is impossible to restrain. It must let off all its venom and run its course. Afterwards, and only afterwards, will we torture ourselves by a life of penance. Having receïved the revelation of sin, having committed it on our own account, we will simply have to expiate in perfect awareness until death. We will pay our debt to God or to the devil. Perhaps we've even paid it in advance? So many prayers and sacrifices since the beginning of time! What of the darkness of original sin, to be redeemed? What of the simple fact of living in this world, in one particular country of the world? Our penance will know no bounds.

Doctor Painchaud is the first to act, pushed by a kind of professional reflex. He tells Sister Julie to lie down. She sobs loudly. The doctor wipes her forehead and face.

"You must sleep. You must. I'm going to give you an injection."

Mother Marie-Clotilde tucks the baby into a flap of her veil. Sister Julie makes no move to take the child. Must not her Master's will be done? As soon as the injection flows in her veins she sinks into contented sleep perfectly exhausted.

Jean Painchaud leans over Sister Julie, although she is already beyond reach. He begs her not to abandon him. He says that the child's birth breaks his heart. He insists upon knowing the father's name. Sister Julie sleeps deeply.

The doctor leaves the convent without a look at the bawling baby. While Mother Marie-Clotilde carries it off, hidden in her veil.

The Lord is my shepherd; I shall not want.
He maketh me to lie down in green pastures:
He leadeth me beside the still waters.
He restoreth my soul.

We must sing loudly, and clearly, with full deployment of the harmonium. Our Superior ordered us to, so that no one in this convent should hear another cry as from a newborn kitten caught within the wall. Permission to return to our cells will be granted only when silence has been completely restored in the house.

Mother Marie-Clotilde has set the baby down on her desk. She stares at it intently. Fascinated and disgusted, she gathers her strength. Recharges herself like an electric battery for an extraordinary expenditure of energy.

Father Flageole is on the other side of the desk beside her. He also looks at the child, impatient to give way to the violence organizing and readying itself within him. While his priest's mind reasons and rationalizes with all its might, inventing the crime and its justification at the same time.

Red, wrinkled, grimacing, with his huge ears, deformed, enormous, neckless head, violet hands, protruding abdomen, frail limbs, gigantic penis. He brings his little arms to his chest and his little thighs to his belly. His chest rises faster and faster. His cries grow ever fainter.

"He looks like a toad," thinks Mother Marie-Clotilde.

"It's the son of Satan," thinks Léo-Z. Flageole. "We're suffocating here. This child gives off an unnatural warmth."

The chaplain is streaming with sweat. He opens the window wide upon the winter night. Picks up handfuls of snow from the windowsill. Covers the child with it. As if trying to extinguish the fires of Hell.

I have given them the demon for communion. Evil is in them now. A new-born child smothered in snow. I have nothing more to do in this house. Mission accomplished. My Master will be pleased. He awaits me outside.

Sister Julie of the Trinity has put on the coarse skirt and jacket she cut from her gray flanelette blanket. On her shorn head, a white kerchief tied under her chin. She has carefully laid the cast-off clothing of the ladies of the Precious Blood on the bed, not wanting to take any part of her religious costume with her.

The system of pulley, ropes and baskets Mother Marie-Clotilde installed in the transom is once again of great help to her. She has only to fasten it all to the window. Fortunately it looks out on the street.

The high sky is full of stars. Newly fallen snow gives off blue reflections. Extraordinary peace. The whole city is asleep. A tall, lean young man dressed in a long, tight-fitting coat, his felt hat drawn over his eyes, awaits Sister Julie in the street.

ALSO BY ANNE HÉBERT,
AUTHOR OF **CHILDREN OF THE BLACK SABBATH**

THE SILENT ROOMS $1.95

by Anne Hébert

The Silent Rooms is Anne Hébert's highly praised novel that won the *Prix France-Canada* when it was first published in French.

Catherine falls in love with Michael, a young pianist who lives in a mansion full of shadows and memories, and leaves with him for Paris where she believes she will finally find freedom. But in Paris she discovers that Michael is cold, aloof, and intent upon imprisoning her in his own fantasies. And when his sister, Lia, appears and moves into the newlyweds' apartment, Catherine learns that she can never be part of their strange world — she has exchanged the prison of her childhood for stifling rooms of elegant decay, where the brother and sister — as perverted by their childhoods as Catherine has been wounded by hers — set out to destroy Catherine and each other.

KAMOURASKA $1.75

by Anne Hébert

Kamouraska — a powerful novel of passion and violence — is based on a true love-triangle story of murder that took place in Quebec during the 1800's. It is the story of Elisabeth d'Aulnieres, who was raised by her mother and three maiden aunts, and who had a youthful but initially happy marriage to the squire of Kamouraska, Antoine de Tassy. Antoine is given to periods of drinking, gambling, whores and the occasional wife-beating — resulting in Elisabeth's return to the watchful care of her aunts, mother and an English doctor, under whose care Elisabeth is placed. A love quickly develops between the two and Elisabeth becomes pregnant. She feigns a reconciliation with her husband, who has now joined her, in an effort to make him believe the child is his, but the threats continue — and the two lovers plot his murder.

USE OUR HANDY ORDER FORM
AT THE BACK OF THIS BOOK . . .

BOOKS TO READ BY MARIAN ENGEL

JOANNE — $1.95

by Marian Engel

Joanne is the story of a Canadian woman in her thirties, with two children, a big house and a straying husband. Written in diary form, it gives a day-by-day account of the break-up of a marriage and how the heroine, humorous, harried and slightly heretical, copes with the changes taking place in her life after her husband leaves. This crisis precipitates a chain of events which leads to a whole new way of life for Joanne and the discovery that a happy life is not only possible but sometimes easier without a husband.

SARAH BASTARD'S NOTEBOOK — $1.50

by Marian Engel

Sarah Porlock, alias the bastard of the title is a wildly disillusioned assistant professor at the University of Toronto. She's an engaging misfit who refuses to apologize for committing adultery or undergoing abortion. How she got that way and why she won't repent are what's happening here, and Ms. Engel is as much interested in defining and depicting an attitude toward life — particularly life in middle class Toronto — as she is in telling a story". — Toronto *Star*.

ONE WAY STREET — $1.50

by Marian Engel

In *One Way Street* we meet another of Marian Engel's heroines, Audrey Moore — intelligent, Canadian, 36 — facts which help her not at all during her sojourn on a Greek Island where she is staying with her estranged husband, a has-been concert pianist with sexual proclivities which do not include Audrey. Although she senses life on the island will be a one-way street for her, the heroine becomes deeply involved with the island's characters and finally takes a Greek lover.

MORE GREAT FICTION FROM

PaperJacks

BADLANDS $2.50
by Robert Kroetsch

Dawe is obsessed, almost mad. He's going down the Red Deer River in the summer of 1916 on a raft with Web, Tune, Grizzly the cook, hunting for dinosaur bones, but this hunt is an obsession, maybe an excuse, which has split him from his wife and daughter back east.

Anne, his daughter, comes to the valley fifty-six years later searching for some reminder of her paleontologist father.

THE WORDS OF MY ROARING $1.95
by Robert Kroetsch

Johnnie J. Backstrom is in trouble. He's running for office in Canadian wheat country during the Great Depression, and it hasn't rained for a long, long time. The times are hard, the people dejected, and Johnnie's chances slim against the wily incumbent — old Doc Murdoch, the very man who delivered Johnnie into the world.

THE STUDHORSE MAN $1.95
by Robert Kroetsch

The Studhorse Man is a Canadian odyssey told by a madman who works naked in a bathtub. The hero is Hazard Lepage, last of the studhorse men, and owner of a superb blue virgin stallion named Poseidon. A fanatical horsebreeder, his passion is to find the perfect mare for his magnificent animal.

HARRIET MARWOOD, GOVERNESS $2.95
by John Glassco

Originally published anonymously in 1955, this book now emerges from under the counter as a pornographic classic. Set in the 1880's, the story deals with a young boy's domination by his beautiful and sadistic governess. Her 'discipline' gradually becomes necessary to him and he grows to manhood equating agony and ecstasy. Harriet Marwood becomes his guardian and then his wife, with full power over a will-less and dependent young man.

IN THE MIDDLE OF A LIFE $1.95
by Richard Wright

In the Middle of a Life covers three days in the life of Freddy Landon, a forty-two-year-old, unemployed greeting-card salesman who lives in a small apartment in one of the older, seedier parts of Toronto. When the novel opens, several things are converging in Landon's life. Not only is he having trouble finding a job ("I'll be frank, Fred — at forty-two you just don't fit into our pension scheme . . .") but his ex-wife and his seventeen-year-old daughter are returning to Toronto after ten years in New York — just when he has become deeply involved in an "affair of the heart" with his neighbour, a middle-aged spinster.

AN ANSWER FROM LIMBO $1.50
by Brian Moore

Brendan Tierney, hack magazine writer, has dreamt for years of writing the great novel he knows is inside him. Goaded into action by the success of an untalented contemporary, he gives up his job and sends his wife out to work, so that he can devote himself completely to writing. In a truly horrifying climax, he learns the full extent of his ruthlessness. "Mr. Moore is surely one of the most versatile and compelling novelists writing today." — *Daily Telegraph*.

ORDER FORM

MAIL SERVICE DEPARTMENT
PAPERJACKS LTD.

330 STEELCASE ROAD EAST
MARKHAM, ONTARIO L3R 2M1
CANADA

No. of Copies	order No.	Title	Price
______	7737-7089-5	AGENCY	$1.95______
______	7737-7043-7	WHITE ESKIMO	1.95______
______	7737-7083-6	TOMORROW WILL BE SUNDAY	1.95______
______	7737-7082-8	THE FOXES OF BEACHY COVE	1.75______
______	7737-7084-3	JOANNE	1.95______

Please add handling charges: 25¢ for one book
50¢ for two or more books ______

Please enclose cheque or money order.
We cannot be responsible for orders containing cash.

TOTAL______

(Please print clearly)

NAME____

ADDRESS______________________________________

CITY____

PROVINCE ____________________ CODE ____________________